Terror in the Dark:
A Collection
of
Horror Stories

by

I0663647

Joshua Griffith

ISBN: 978-1-7350784-5-8

Cover art by SelfPubBookCovers.com/ ktarrier

Contact Joshua Griffith on Facebook

Follow him on Twitter

Or on BookBub

Table of Contents

The Maze of Shadows

Harbinger's Orders

A Bully's Comeuppance

A Watery Grave

The Ghost and the Zombie

Tales from the Fae War

A Gremlin's Antics

A New Beginning

The Invitation

The Maze of Shadows

(A short story from the Yonuh universe)

Sara waved goodbye to her friends as she exited the little dive bar. It was getting late and it was time to leave her coven after another great night of drinking and blathery exchanges. The witch enjoyed the cool downtown air that swept in from the Columbia River.

The nightlife of Portland was always lively; people wanted to do nothing more than to have fun and be merry after the terrible plague took out most of the world's population. Most of the local businesses and homeowners used solar panels so, despite the lack of a power grid, many who live in Oregon were prepared for the apocalypse. Especially Portland.

The witch knew that she had to be on her guard—rumors of paramilitary teams hunting down supernatural creatures was the talk of tonight's meeting.

But that's all they were, just rumors and no evidence to show that they existed, but they couldn't deny the disappearances that had occurred. Several coven members were absent from the last three gatherings, so suspicions were running high.

Sara was expecting her friend, Raven Moonrose, to come along with her so she could introduce her to the coven, but when she got to Raven's house, she saw that it had been set on fire. The witch searched the charred, skeletal wreckage but didn't find Raven's body. The only thing that seemed out of place were the many heavy footprints from combat boots along with the slim bootprints that belonged to her friend.

Could someone actually be hunting us?

Sara shivered as she wrapped her dark blue cloak tightly to her body. Despite the cool night air, a chill ran over her, which Sara couldn't attribute to the weather. Something was amiss, though she couldn't quite figure out what exactly it was.

As she strolled in the direction of the Waterfront Park, Sara opened her senses to search for who or what exactly was following her. She had protections in the form of a talisman and several enchanted rings that would alert her to danger. The problem was that was the extent of the power that those items held.

Sara's boots click-clacked on the wet sidewalk, her path dimly lit from the ambient light from the full moon. She smiled at the notion of getting sky-clad, dancing in the grass under the beauty of the moon, possibly taking a dip in the majestic Columbia River. The witch also imagined Yonuh dancing with her.

Sara contently sighed at the memory of the shape-shifter that the community referred to as Yonuh the Meat Bear. The Native American got the moniker because he bartered some high quality and valuable meats from the different animals that he hunted and butchered himself. Most often, Yonuh would simply give it away, which surprised many of vendors who had booths here on the waterfront and at the Clackamas Mall Market.

After the plague hit, fresh game was considered a premium item because of its scarcity and the fact that not many people around knew how to properly butcher animals. It was like going into a grocery store, before the plague, and paying ten thousand dollars for a pack of gum.

Yonuh did this so regularly all the vendors, despite his protesting it by saying that he was just giving back to the community, gave the shape-shifter credit. She didn't quite understand the man and his way of thinking, but his touch always elicited a warm, comforting feeling. Another strange thing about his touch was that it caused Sara's core to become aroused from whatever magic Yonuh was naturally putting off, which made her nibble on her bottom lip.

The things that I would do to that man, especially if he were here right now…

Her erotic thoughts were interrupted by the interloper in the shadows, obviously stalking her. Her hand slipped into a pocket in her purple vest, fingering her oak wand. Sara had a vague feeling that her stalker wasn't human, and in these lawless times the witch wanted to keep her virtue intact from the many predators lurking about everywhere. She looked to her left and to her right, her senses tingling as the entity eluded her.

It's toying with me, the witch fumed as she extracted her weapon from her pocket, holding it out and preparing for a fight.

"I know you're there," Sara growled. "Show yourself, you coward, and I might go easy on you."

The tip of her wand glowed with power as the witch turned in circles, hunting for her quarry. Sara could see something just on the edge of her peripheral vision, teasing her. Her cobalt eyes flared brightly with her heightened emotional state as her eyes locked on a shadowy figure.

As she fired a magical blast at the unknown entity, Sara heard a whoosh of air from behind her and then everything in her vision faded into darkness as she collapsed.

The witch tentatively opened her eyes, the back of her head throbbing in pain. She winced as she touched the base of her skull.

What happened to me? Sara wondered as she noticed something wet and sticky on the tips of her fingers. Unable to focus her eyes on her surroundings, Sara placed her fingers to her nose and a metallic aroma assailed her senses. She crinkled her nose in disgust. The witch couldn't quite recall what happened to her. The last thing she recalled was walking towards the waterfront.

Now she was here, wherever this place was, and it filled her with a sense of dread. She was lying prone on her side on what felt like an icy road. Puffs of foggy breath escaped her quivering lips as her body quaked from the freezing environment. Sara surveyed her surroundings with bleary eyes, trying to discern her location. A light barely lit a long alleyway.

Everything appeared black. The walls and the stone street glistened as though it had recently rained, but there were no visible puddles.

She gingerly sat up, wincing in pain as she wrapped her arms across her chest. Sara peered down at her body, panic spiking through her mind.

Where're my clothes??

Her body was covered in bruises and lacerations. Her protective rings, talisman, and wand were gone.

"Oh Gods!" Sara cried out, her breaths coming in rapid, shallow succession as a full-blown panic attack tightly squeezed her chest. She heard the sound of metal scraping across a hard surface as she lifted herself to her feet. Her eyes darted everywhere but couldn't find the source of scraping as it got louder and closer.

The witch put her hands against the cold wall. She leaned forward to bolt as adrenaline coursed through her body. Her mind screamed for her to flee but her legs were frozen in place. The metal scraping grew louder, and in the blink of an eye two shackles clamped down on Sara's wrists.

The chains attached to the shackles snapped taut as they hoisted her up the icy-cold wall. Sara's heart pounded so hard she thought it would burst out of her chest. She frantically looked up but couldn't see anything. The chains stretched up into the darkened sky — if it was the sky — and faded to nothing. It was as if the chains had sprung from the darkness like snakes.

"Who are you?" the witch blurted out in the darkness as she cried. "What do you want from me?"

Somewhere in the distance, she heard a scream that was followed by a low, guttural growl that sent a chill up her spine.

What is happening?

This place reminded her of the Shanghai Tunnels that she loved traveling through as a means of escaping the chaos during the plague outbreak. Only, this place was more expansive and creepier. Her attention snapped back down at the road beneath her.

Her mouth gaped open but no sound left her throat. The witch knew that it wasn't human, definitely not a part of the rumored paramilitary group.

Whatever it was, it caused her to go completely still as it approached. The creature stood at least eight feet tall and walked with a hunched back. Its flesh was a putrid green with bulbous yellow pustules oozing with every movement. Its slim arms glistened in the dim light, a thick liquid substance dripping from the tentacles that snaked around from its back. Sara could do nothing but dangle in the air, her naked body vulnerable and at its mercy.

She was petrified with terror. Her bottom lip quivered as the creature locked its slanted black eyes with hers, daring her to scream. It snaked up one of its slimy tentacles, snaring her left foot. She trembled as the thing turned her body, meticulously examining her. Her anxiety skyrocketed as the creature eyed her like a predator ready to pounce.

"Please, just let me go," Sara pleaded.

This seemed to amuse her captor, and it let out an eerie laugh that sounded like a swarm of flies caught in a food processor.

The creature tsked, "You're not much to look at, but at least you're fit and trim."

Sara growled in disgust, "You've no room to talk, freak. Now let me go or —"

"Or what, witch?" The creature cut her off, amused by her bravado. "You'll spit nasty names at me? I will release you from your bindings, but first I must lay out the ground rules."

Sara narrowed her eyes suspiciously. "Ground rules? For what?"

The creature chuckled as it let go of her foot. It wiggled its tentacles in the air, and the chains lowered Sara back down to the ground. As her feet touched down, the witch's confidence faltered now that she was facing the creature. She stifled a cry as it towered over her, its hot breath cascading over her body like a river of raw sewage. The creature drew its lips back in a malicious grin, revealing several rows of jagged, sharp teeth.

"If it were up to me, I'd be devouring you right now, but I'm not allowed to do that, not yet..."

Sara gulped. "What do you want from me?"

"You've been selected to partake in the Maze of Shadows," the creature announced as it leaned in close to her ear. "You're here for our amusement, and trust me when I say that if you don't make it to the white room, you *will* die."

Sara blanched as the creature moved back into her vision, reveling in her terror.

The creature mused, "Being fit and athletic might give you a sporting chance, but if it doesn't..." It craned its head in the direction of the sound of a man shrieking in agony, "You *will* be screaming the same way that man just did."

Sara's mind was reeling so much that she barely noticed that her arms were no longer dangling above her head as the chains loosened.

She closed her eyes, not daring to look at the creature as she asked, "How am I supposed to get to the white room when I'm chained up like this?"

The creature gagged several times and then Sara felt something hot and wet splatter her feet. She looked down and saw the contents of the creature's stomach. Among the acrid sludge were partial human remains and a tiny sliver of metal — a key that looked ornate with a serpent's head, yet corroded.

As the creature shuffled backwards, it motioned to the pavement to her left. "You have two minutes to free yourself, get dressed in the clothing I've generously provided, and run as though your life depended on it… because it does. If you fail to do this, then you will be eaten alive…or worse."

"What can be worse than being eaten alive?" the witch asked with concern, nervously biting her trembling bottom lip.

The creature chuckled. "A word of advice: trust no one in here. That will get you killed quickly. Get to the white room and you will be granted freedom as your reward."

As it shuffled away, the creature called over its hunched shoulder, "You'd best free yourself. I sense something deadly is heading this way...and it's hungry."

The witch dropped to her knees and tentatively plucked the slimy key from the vomit. She crinkled her nose as the acidic odor of half-digested flesh wafted up, burning her eyes. A howl from somewhere nearby set her nerves on edge.

She frantically worked on unlocking the shackles. As she unlocked the first shackle, she yelped and dropped the key. She glanced down at her fingers to see that they were burning. The stomach acid had eaten away at her flesh! Another howl echoed down the dark corridor. This time it sounded closer, followed by a barrage of snarls. Sara quickly reached for the key, gritting her teeth as the key caused her skin to sizzle.

After several panicked attempts, she managed to slip it into the keyholes of each of her restraints. The shackles fell off her wrists as the sound of something scraping in tandem with the snarls reached her ears. She reached over and quickly snatched up the pile of form-fitting clothing the creature had left for her and slipped it on.

Sara stood up and sprinted as quickly as she could manage. Eyes darting everywhere, the witch hoped that whatever stalked her would be slow and lumbering. She dared a peek over her shoulder and saw a massive silhouette. It was lurking around the spot where she had been restrained.

It snatched up one of the shackles, sniffing it carefully. Its head jerked in her direction and the witch almost froze as its blood-red eyes glowed. The beast howled as it bounded after her like it had been fired from a cannon. Sara shrieked as she came up to a "T" section of the maze, unsure which way to take. The beast lunged for her, snapping its jaws mere inches from her neck.

The witch darted to her left and rounded the corner, but the beast swiped a massive muscular arm at her. She cried out in pain as razor-sharp claws sliced into the small of her back. A booming thud and a painful grunt caused Sara to glance over her shoulder.

Through teary eyes, she could see the beast on the ground. Its furry head was split open with blood pouring out, a result of its head-on collision with the concrete wall. The witch didn't care to find out if it was alive or dead. She ran around another corner and was greeted with a dead end.

Panting through gritted teeth, she turned around to go back the way she came. Unease crept into her mind as she peered around the corner. The beast was still lying where it fell; she observed that it was breathing but unmoving as blood continued to ooze out from its self-inflicted wound.

Sara nervously slipped past the beast as she winced in pain from her wounds. She held her breath, worried that she might wake the beast. Just as she got past it, she heard a heavy snort.

She jerked her head and saw that the beast was eyeing her. Its eyes pierced her soul, with malicious intent.

The witch sprinted away from the beast as it tried to lunge for her. It was badly hurt, so she managed to escape it easily. She kept glancing over her shoulder, expecting to see the hairy monstrosity closing in on her, but all she saw was the darkness of the maze.

She turned the corner and ended up colliding with someone, knocking them both to the ground. Sara scooted back and out of reach. To her relief, it was a person. The woman was wearing a smudged-up wedding dress. The other woman cowered away as she asked, "Who are you?"

Wearily, Sara replied, "I'm Sara; what's your name?"

"S-Savannah. I've been stuck here for I don't know how long." She nervously looked around and then added, "So much death. I don't think I'm going to make it out of here alive..."

"The feeling is mutual," Sara stated as she stood up and walked past Savannah, but the other woman grabbed her leg.

"Not that way!" Savannah shrieked.

The witch pulled away from the woman's grip and jogged forward, feeling slightly more confident, but only just. She flinched slightly as Savannah walked in step beside her, the witch's eyes cautiously scanning everywhere.

Sara felt bad for the traumatized woman and wanted to keep her safe, but that didn't mean she was going to let her guard down. As they trekked through the maze, the witch noticed the color of the walls had changed. Instead of black they were now red, like blood.

"I wonder if the color means anything..." Sara said out loud.

"Yes, it does. It means we're getting deeper into the maze," Savannah answered.

Sara glanced at her with suspicion. "How do you know?"

"The thing that released me into the maze told me all about it. I didn't believe her when she said that I was in a maze. The place I started from was a small white room that had four doors. Each one represents the colors of the maze which are red, black, yellow, and white."

Sara stopped Savannah. "You were in the white room? Why did you come this way?"

"Because she told me to pick a door or I would be killed in that room. So I chose the yellow door, and I've been roaming in this maze ever since," Savannah replied with a haunted gaze.

"Mine told me that I had to get to the white room if I wanted to live. You were at the exit and didn't even know it."

Savannah gasped. "Really? That bitch told me that if I opened the white door, I would be dead because there was a nasty, hungry creature behind it. As soon as she left, I heard a terrible sound coming from that door, so I ran…"

"Do you know the way back to the white room?" Sara asked hopefully.

"I think so. I went out the yellow door, and I walked through the red part of the maze before literally running into you in the black part."

Moans and screams in the distance filled the witch with trepidation, her determination wavering as her mind played off those sounds, creating a number of horrible scenarios.

All ending bloody. Savannah surveyed the maze, trying to discern the route she had taken when, all of a sudden, a man wearing jogging shorts and a blue blazer ran by. A moment later, a slick amber goo flowed after the man.

Savannah ran ahead, squealing in excitement as she pointed, "That's the corridor we need to take! I remember seeing that slimy thing before. Just don't step in the trail it leaves behind."

"Why?" Sara asked as she rounded the corner to catch up with Savannah. "Will it kill me?"

She gently smacked the witch on the shoulder playfully. "No, nothing like that. Think of it as a motion detector. You step on it and you end up calling that blob thing down there right to you."

Sara looked down at the opposite end of the corridor and saw the man trapped by the goo. From what she could see this creature was amorphous, manipulating its body into whatever form it desired. It was translucent, its amber hue making it slightly easier to see through.

It had completely encircled the man with its body, daring him to try an escape attempt. The man leapt over the goo, clearing it easily. As he landed, it ensnared him. The man howled in pain as he watched his flesh melt away, then all his muscles and tendons.

Even his bones dissolved into nothing. He fell forward, smacking his jaw on the hard floor. The goo pooled up and engulfed its victim. The man frantically squirmed inside the creature as he slowly melted away into nothing.

Sara gagged several times at the sight of the man being digested into oblivion before she emptied the contents of her stomach. As it spattered on the floor, food particles ended up in the slime trail at her feet.

Savannah hissed as she ran away, "Stupid girl! I told you not to touch the slime."

Sara wiped her mouth with the back of her hand, then heard a low gurgling sound reverberating through the corridor. She glanced at the gooey creature and saw that it was rushing towards her like a fast-flowing river of syrup.

She bolted down the corridor, trying to keep an eye on Savannah. Every turn she took, Sara could barely catch a glimpse of that dingey white dress slipping out of sight.

Damn, she's fast!

Her heart was pounding like it was ready to explode from her chest as her adrenaline kicked it into overdrive. She wanted to stop, her lungs screaming for respite. To do so now would mean certain death as the goo creature kept up its unyielding pace.

The witch noticed that the maze's colors had changed from red to yellow. Despite her entire body screaming for her to collapse, Sara used this to motivate herself to keep moving. She went left down a small corridor and was greeted by the sight of a white wall with a yellow door.

Sara figured that Savannah must have made it inside the white room already, but now she worried that she might have locked it or barricaded the door for her own safety. The goo creature shot a piece of itself forward and it scraped Sara's right arm, instantly burning away her skin.

She cried out in pain but didn't dare stop. Sara noticed a shadow looming all around her. She glanced up and saw the goo creature had managed to throw most of its body into the air, like a supernatural tsunami wave of digestive death.

As the creature came crashing down all around her, Sara dove ahead and rolled several times before she was stopped by a wall. The goo creature covered the corridor like a bomb had gone off.

Sara scrambled to her feet as the goo creature formed a massive head that glared at her with empty, menacing eyes. It let out a booming growl as it launched its head straight at the witch.

She yanked the yellow door open and slammed it behind her, narrowly escaping the goo creature. She heard it let out a gurgling roar as it smashed against the door several times, but the door never budged.

The witch slid down the door and collapsed from exhaustion, panting hard as she tried to catch her breath. The floor was cold but she welcomed it as a comfort, knowing she had bested two monsters and this fucking maze. She slid her knees up to her chest and slumped her head down, crying as all the pain she'd endured was coming to the forefront.

The cuts that ran along her back stung more now than they had earlier, her sweat seeping into them.

The cuts probably opened up more during my marathon run, she mused.

Sara didn't want to examine the injury to her right arm. After seeing what the goo monster did to that poor guy, she was afraid what her wound would look like after getting brushed by it.

She closed her eyes as she ran her fingers over the wound, and shuddered. It felt like there was a small trench of skin and muscle missing. Tears streamed down her cheeks as she got up the nerve to look.

It looked worse than she imagined. A chunk of her flesh was missing. She could see that it hadn't bled at all; the blood vessels had been cauterized and the remaining muscles and tendons were singed. Her lips quivered as she sobbed. All she wanted to do was to go home.

Where's Savannah? Did she get turned around and miss the white room?

The witch wasn't about to leave this room, not with that angry goo creature lurking outside.

She glanced around the room and saw that everything was the purest white she had ever seen. The only exceptions were three doors.

One was red, on the opposite wall. The other one was black, set in the wall to her right. The white door was to her left, beckoning to her to walk through it. There was a long white table in the middle of the room that had a flashing red light at one end of it.

The witch pulled herself up off the floor, all her muscles demanding more respite. She timidly walked over to the table, her curiosity piqued. She saw that there was a small console attached at the end of the table.

The flashing light was actually a button set next to a miniature speaker. Above it, the words *PRESS ME* were stenciled in black paint. Sara cautiously pressed the red button and a familiar voice called out from the speaker.

"I see that my favorite fodder has made it to the white room. Well done! In a moment, the white room will spin around and around and all the doors will become white. Don't you just love a good shell game, little fodder? Pick the right door and freedom is your prize! Pick the wrong door and you will end up back in the maze, aimlessly wandering once more. So observe well and choose wisely. Who knows, you might beat the odds and win! Three of the four doors lead to certain death, so no pressure, my little fodder. Let the room-shift begin!"

The doors instantly shifted their colors and were all white, the blood stains covering the yellow door washing away before her unbelieving eyes. Sara was smacked hard with vertigo as the walls and floor shifted and spun around in opposite directions. She fell to her knees hard as she closed her eyes.

Oh Gods, make it stop!

Suddenly the room came to a creaking stop, causing her to tumble over. She sat up slowly, allowing her equilibrium to return. She grabbed hold of the white table to get up to a standing position.

The voice on the radio chuckled devilishly, "Open one of the doors and discover your fate, little fodder."

Sara took a deep breath to calm down, but it didn't help. Her anxiety refused to yield as she focused on each door, hoping that one would give away a clue. The only reason she'd gotten here was by sheer dumb luck and the help of Savannah.

She should be here with me, the witch thought.

She walked to one of the doors with trepidation, turned the doorknob, and prayed that the goo creature wasn't waiting for her. As she opened the door, all she could see was a blinding light and nothing else.

The witch shielded her eyes with her hands as she walked towards the light, but then she felt someone grab her from behind and forcefully restrain her. Sara kicked as hard as she could, but no matter how many times she hit the person behind her they didn't let go. The witch groaned in pain as something sharp sank into her neck. She tried once more to escape, but her strength had ebbed away.

Through the blinding door, the hideous host that greeted her at the beginning of the maze walked in with a smile spread across the expanse of its visage.

It clapped its tentacles together joyously as it neared Sara. "You did it, little fodder! You chose the correct door. Congratulations. How does it feel to be a winner? Be truthful now, we're all dying to know."

Sara weakly replied, "If that's the right door…then why aren't you…letting me go? You said…I could go…free if I…picked the right one…"

"Let you go free? I never said that." The creature chuckled as it slithered a tentacle down the side of her face, causing her to flinch. "I told you that freedom would be your prize...big difference. If you had asked me what freedom in the Maze of Shadows meant, I would've told you?"

"Shall I place her on the table now?" a familiar female voice asked beside Sara's ear.

Sara was lifted like she weighed nothing and placed on the table. The female leaned forward into her view and instantly Sara recognized her.

It was Savannah.

Her mouth was covered in blood as she flashed a fang-filled smile. Her eyes were a burnt yellow with a sliver of black streaking the middle. Her skin was now covered in scales, like a snake.

She got inches from Sara's face and slowly ran her forked tongue over the witch's lips. "She's delicious and strong. I'm sure she'll survive."

"I believe you may be right, Savannah." The tentacled creature stood just out of Sara's sight and admonished the witch, "I did warn you not to trust anyone in the maze, and yet you latched on to Savannah here like a lifeline. Did it not occur to you that not everyone in the Maze of Shadows was fodder like you? I suppose it's easy to think that all the *'monsters'* in here would look the part."

Sara made a futile attempt to move her body. "Why…can't I…move…?"

Savannah purred as she nipped at her earlobe. "My love bite has a neurotoxin in it that causes paralysis. Pretty cool, huh? One bite and I can do whatever I wish to you as you watch helplessly."

Sara winced as the host snaked one of its tentacles through her hair and hoisted her up to eye her. "A useful skill to have for what we do to all who make it to the white room."

Sara's lips trembled, but she was unable to speak.

"I should've gotten the first bite on her!" a male voice growled. "Especially after what she did to me, Kryton!"

Sara had her head turned for her so she could see the newcomer in the room. A cold sweat broke out over her body as she gazed upon the hairy beast that had chased her in the maze. Its head was still split open, but appeared to be mending quickly.

Sara's pulse quickened as it approached the table, its eyes glaring at her with murderous intent. It snarled and growled as it roughly grabbed her ankles and spat out, "I should kill you now for leaving me like that!"

"Ah, ah, ah, Trevor," Kryton admonished with a stern gaze. "She made it here, so there will be none of that. You should've killed her out in the maze when you had the chance. It's not her fault that you injured yourself during the hunt. You may bite her once, but that's all you'll get at this point."

Trevor snarled, but obeyed as he lifted one of her legs and sank his massive jaws into the side of her thigh.

Sara could only moan in pain as she was made to watch. Trevor eyed her with hatred as he viciously ripped away a good portion of muscle. He made sure that she witnessed him devour it slowly.

"Sorry, but my venom doesn't dull the senses." Savannah patted her on the shoulder. She looked up at the tentacle creature and asked, "Shall we begin, Kryton?"

"Yes. Go let Bob in," Kryton cheerfully answered. "I'm sure he's eager to see this one again!"

The witch watched as Savannah slithered to one of the doors. She still wore the dingey wedding dress, but the rest of her figure was that of a serpentine creature with no legs.

As Savannah opened the door, she smirked back at Sara as the goo creature poured into the white room. Bob shifted into a translucent humanoid shape as he walked up to the table. Kryton smiled at him and announced, "She's ready for you to grant her freedom, Bob."

Oh, Gods! Sara mentally shouted, wishing that she could escape. *I don't want to be eaten alive!*

Trevor cackled while shaking his massive head, as if he read her mind. "Stupid girl, your ignorance knows no bounds. He wouldn't allow me to kill you, so what makes you think Bob here would get that honor over me?"

The witch could only watch as Bob enveloped her. She screamed as every bone in her body shattered and splintered, shifting into different, unnatural positions. Her neck elongated to the point that she could watch her own body transform.

She felt something pushing out of her tailbone and growing in size. More snaps and cracking occurred as her nose and jaw protruded forward like a snout. Her hands grew to twice their normal size and the tips of her fingers had lethal talons. Her back painfully bulged before her skin ripped open and new appendages emerged. Sara prayed that Bob would dissolve her into nothing. Nothing was worth this pain and torture.

Bob spat her out onto the floor. Sara sniffled and shook from the cold waves that her body was experiencing. She looked up and saw Bob as he shifted his body to mimic a mirror.

She was horrified by the sudden changes and wasn't sure if what she was seeing was real. The pain she felt was real as she stood up to examine the gruesome additions. She had grown the tail of a scorpion and now had wings like a bat. Her skin shimmered in the light like she was covered in glitter.

Her clothing seemed to mesh with the transformation and fit snuggly, somehow. Sara cried as she hugged her arms around her chest, her new wings mimicking this as they cocooned the rest of her body.

Kryton clapped his tentacles. "You survived the transformation and have been granted the freedom you deserve. Welcome, Sara, into our family! Our latest addition to the Maze of Shadows. You will live forever as one of us, as we gather more fodder for our entertainment...and sustenance!"

Harbinger's Orders

(The Reset Series)

In an undisclosed facility along the border of Russia and China, 1980.

The ancient deity stood up and adjusted his celestial garments as the occupants of the room collapsed to the floor. He placed his hands on Jasmine's limp body and turned it into ash in an instant.

As the denizens of the secret military facility whimpered, Harbinger created a magical sphere and placed it on the dead witch's remains. The ancient god rotated his index finger over the sphere, causing a small vortex that pulled Jasmine's remains inside.

When he was satisfied that every bit of her remains were inside, Harbinger picked up the sphere and made it vanish.

"Why do you need my ashes…?" The ghost of the dead witch asked as it hovered next to the deity.

He turned and walked out the door. "I need it to weave the protection into your kind.

The ones that have supernatural gifts shall bear witness to the Reset and set the world right once more. You, on the other hand, I'll transform into something better than a mere ghost."

"Will it be painful…?" Jasmine asked tentatively.

"All forms of transformation involve a lot of pain in order for growth to occur. This will be no different for you, because it will take time for your new form to come to fruition."

The guards at the door were unconscious as the deity stepped out in the hallway. Harbinger glanced at his ghostly companion and asked, "Where exactly are the prisoners in this facility housed?"

Jasmine thought for a moment and shrugged her ethereal shoulders. *"I'm not sure... I wasn't made privy to the location of the holding cells...I summoned a few entities but they were all taken away in shackles..."*

The deity groaned with annoyance but kept walking. Several soldiers stepped out of the elevator and froze. Seeing the ancient deity unbound and unescorted caused the men to unholster their firearms.

"Hold it right there! Where's the general? What did you do to him?" one soldier barked out.

"Resting in that room. Now, if you will excuse me, I have other matters to tend to at the moment," Harbinger replied, sounding bored by the conversation.

As the ancient deity moved, the soldiers opened fire on him. The bullets hit their mark, but fell harmlessly to the floor.

The ancient deity looked at the stunned men coldly. "Do you truly want a fight, or simply wish to waste your primitive projectiles on me?"

One of the soldiers rushed forward and smashed the butt of his pistol against Harbinger's face. The ancient deity waited patiently as more blows rained down on him before the handle cracked and became deformed.

The god appeared mildly amused as he asked, "Are you done?"

The soldier was perplexed as he examined his sidearm. The ancient deity snapped his fingers, instantly breaking the necks of the other soldiers. He grabbed his stunned assailant by the throat and hoisted him off the ground with little effort and menacingly asked, "Where are the other prisoners located in this hovel?"

"I'll..." the man gasped. "I'll never... tell... Go to...Hell, freak..."

Harbinger chuckled coldly as he brought the soldier mere inches from his unmarred visage and stated, "You mortals and your limited knowledge of everything. Don't bother being brave. I'm going to extract the information I seek straight from your pathetic brain. I'd tell you that it won't hurt, but that's a lie and I despise lies."

The ancient deity placed three fingers on the soldier's forehead, causing the man to scream like thousands of small, cold spikes were piercing his skull. The helpless soldier shook violently as his body seized, foam oozing from the corners of his lips and blood trickling from his nose and ears.

Harbinger flung the man hard against the concrete wall, his body impacting it so hard that little fissures appeared.

"Useless thug," the ancient deity muttered as Jasmine appeared next to him. She bowed her head and meekly stated, *"Follow me, Master. I know where the prisoners are being kept..."*

"No need to use formality with me, Jasmine," Harbinger grumbled with an eye roll. "I'm not your master. More like your evolutionary guide. I somewhat know their location, but his brain melted before I could get a precise fix. Lead the way, little witchling."

The ghost pointed at the dead soldier. *"Take his ID... It will unlock many doors..."*

"These primitive devices can't bar my way," Harbinger replied with a sneer as he opened his hand and made the ID fly into his grip. "Since these fools want to unleash numerous plagues on this world, I'll allow this structure to remain serviceable. My plan needs this in order to occur."

Jasmine beckoned him to enter the elevator as she passed through the closed door. The deity swiped the badge over the electronic lock and pressed the button. The witch's spirit greeted him as the door slid open with a metallic grind.

"Press the button on the bottom of the panel for sublevel three... Many creatures are warehoused down there..."

"What do you mean by that?" Harbinger asked as he magically pressed the button, causing it to light up.

"It means that the prisoners are being packed in tight quarters... Too many beings and so little room to roam... I never knew of their miserable plight..." Jasmine stated sadly.

"Your ignorance is barely an excuse, but seeing how you were treated here by these men makes up for it. These cretins have many hidden secrets and agendas. It will not end well for them or their masters."

The door screeched closed and the elevator lurched slightly as it shifted into motion. Jasmine's gaze fell to the floor as she said, *"Forgive me for not knowing... I summoned some of them using the rift, but never knew what happened to the entities afterwards..."*

"Noted," the ancient deity replied flatly. "If absolution is what you seek, you'll get none from me. You can make amends for your role in all of this by becoming the Protector."

"I'm a ghost, remember?" Jasmine bitterly bit out. *"How can I protect anyone when I can no longer interact with the physical realm..."*

"As I said earlier, you're a key piece to my plan which will save many lives," Harbinger replied with a cold chuckle. "You have a choice to make. Work for me and I will re-form you into the being you need to be in order to accomplish this task. If not, you can remain a ghost and haunt this facility forever. Maybe you can scare off the people here, but I doubt it."

"Not much of a choice," Jasmine flatly replied.

"Indeed," Harbinger replied as the elevator dinged and the door scraped open, "but it's a choice you must make. I can always find another, if need be. I wouldn't be upset with you, so wipe that thought from your mind."

He stepped out of the elevator and into a dark, damp corridor. Water dripped from the metal pipes that ran along the concrete ceiling. Harbinger could sense the other entities and moved down the winding corridor.

Several maintenance men in hardhats and coveralls were working on a section of the leaky piping as the ancient deity approached. One of the men noticed Harbinger as he shined his flashlight at him and asked, "Who are you and what's your purpose down here?"

"That's of no concern to you, child. Just keep doing what you're doing and all will be fine," the ancient deity replied calmly as he kept walking.

"Child?!" the man bellowed. He rushed up to the deity, jabbing him in the chest. "I'm the foreman down here and I demand that you show some ID, buddy, or — "

"Or what? You'll shine your deadly electric torch in my eyes?" Harbinger grew several feet taller than the man, causing the foreman to lose his resolve as well as his flashlight. "I tire of you humans and your pathetic sense of self-importance."

With a snap of his finger the foreman's body exploded, caking the walls and other maintenance men in blood and gore. All but one of the men fled, screaming. The ancient deity approached the man, pausing beside him and asking, "Do you wish to join your fleeing friends, or the foreman?"

"Doesn't matter what I choose," the man said flatly. "I'm a dead man either way. Kill me now, or let my body do it."

Harbinger's gaze fell on the lone maintenance man, freezing him on the ladder that he stood on. He cocked his head and said, "I see what you speak of, Jacob. You're not long for this world, are you?"

"No, I'm not. Do what you must," Jacob replied stoically.

The ancient deity put a hand on Jacob's head, causing the man's body to quake, but he never fell from the ladder. After a minute,

Harbinger released his hold over Jacob and said coldly, "The cancer is gone. I only did it because I see that you have the gift of a seer in you. I suggest that you hone this skill, because you're going to need it."

Jacob stepped off the ladder, feeling a bit woozy, but managed to stay upright as he leaned against the wall. He looked up at the ancient deity and asked, "Why heal me? Why not let me die?"

"That can still be arranged, mortal," Harbinger replied, his black eyes pulsating. "But you already knew that I wouldn't do it because you have already foreseen it. You won't escape the calamity that is to come, so kill yourself or help others who have gifts when the time comes. I truly don't care."

"I've done my best to hide it because I don't want to be added to the experimentations that have been going on down here," Jacob replied with a shudder. He pointed down the corridor at the red door and said, "That door leads the way to the many atrocities that are happening in this place as we speak. I've had to do numerous repairs in the many rooms past that door."

"Why don't you simply leave this place?" the ancient deity asked.

"In a body bag is the only way one leaves this place," Jacob replied. "This is a top-secret facility. They keep us grunts on a tight lease and under constant surveillance. If I try to skip the country, my life is forfeit. I know this because I've seen it happen to others, with my gift."

"*Jacob speaks the truth...*" Jasmine said as she hovered next to the ancient deity. "*It's all in the contract that we signed when we were brought here... They don't want their secrets revealed...*"

Harbinger grunted as he moved forward, heading straight for the red door. He swiped the ID over the electronic lock and the door opened. The ancient deity could feel vast amounts of residual pain and anguish the moment he stepped over the threshold.

Jacob ran up and joined his side, holding a red plastic card. "Take this. It will open all the doors in this facility. It will also keep them from tracking the ID that you're using. It's my way of saying thanks for curing me."

"On one condition," Harbinger said.

"Name it," Jacob quickly replied.

"You keep it and lead the way. I am doing my best *not* to level this facility. Using these cards is grating on my nerves. You will be under my protection if you do this for me, Jacob."

The maintenance man nodded as he went ahead of the deity. Jasmine flew next to Harbinger and asked, "*Is he one who will be liberated from this place?*"

"It all depends on what he chooses to do. Humanity is a terrible disease upon this world. This place serves as a small sample of the cruelty that humans can unleash on both themselves and the environment. Humanity is doomed, but a select few will ensure that this planet survives," the ancient deity coldly remarked as he neared the first set of doors.

Harbinger placed his hand on the door and closed his eyes. A slight sneer covered his visage. "Hybridization. Genetic manipulation. How original."

"I-I never knew," Jacob stammered, then he asked, "Do you want the door open?"

"No, it's just as empty as the amount of compassion is in this facility." The ancient deity opened his eyes. He could hear someone or something coming from three doors away. Harbinger pointed at the door and ordered, "That one. Open it."

The maintenance guy nodded and briskly walked over to the door. Jacob could barely hear muted moaning coming from inside. He glanced at the god nervously. "I don't think I'm going to like what I find in here."

"All the more reason to open it. You need to truly *see*, seer, to understand," Harbinger said flatly.

Jacob gulped loudly, his throat parched as he scanned his badge on the lock. When he pushed the door open, the muted moaning turned into a frenzied, ear-piercing scream. A green-haired female was vertically strapped to a metal table. She had no clothing on, but had numerous tubes inserted into various parts of her body. Pieces of her flesh had been surgically removed, exposing the muscles beneath.

Three men and one woman in lab coats were busy jotting down notes on their clipboards, while another man in a scrub uniform, holding a scalpel in his blood-soaked, gloved hand, was shining a little light into her bleary eyes.

He glanced at the door and shouted, "You're not supposed to be in here, boy! When we have a need for your services, we'll let you know. Now leave!"

"I can't. I have orders to be in here!" Jacob shouted as he pointed at the female. "Who is she, and what are you doing to her?"

"It doesn't concern you, boy!" the surgeon bellowed as he angrily marched towards the maintenance guy. "On whose authority—"

"*Mine!*" Harbinger growled, loud enough to cause everyone in the room to pause as he entered the room. He reached out and grabbed the surgeon by the neck and hoisted him effortlessly off the floor. One of the other scientists managed to run to the wall behind the screaming female prisoner and pressed the alarm button.

"Security is on their way!" one of the scientists stated as the alarm system rang out overhead. "I suggest that you put Dr. Rivera down and surrender."

The door slammed shut as other workers attempted to flee. No matter how much they tried to get it to open, the door didn't budge. The ancient deity glared at the men, his eyes glowing, and he replied, "What's the hurry? You're going to tell me what I want to know, or you'll find yourselves in *her* place."

"It-It's — " Dr. Rivera choked out, "classified!"

"I'm growing tired of that statement," Harbinger said as he grew in size and height, causing the other scientists to freak out. "Release her or I'll do it myself. You won't like it if I do it."

The ancient deity squeezed his hand, causing the surgeon's head to pop off like a champagne cork. Blood sprayed all around as the head bounced on the floor. Harbinger threw the body at the scientists and said, "Your choice, bugs."

The one worker behind the female pulled the tubes out of her body, his hands shaking. "She's not going to stop screaming. The drugs that are coursing through her system are causing it so—"

"Shut your mutant monkey mouth and free her!" Harbinger bellowed, causing the other scientists to move to assist. "You humans enjoy playing God and yet don't know what to do when one actually shows up. Your lives matter not to me, but hers does!"

As banging on the other side of the door commenced, the scientist who hit the alarm looked at the ancient deity with wide eyes. "You're the one that the witch summoned tonight? Why are you doing this? Why are you still here?"

Harbinger didn't acknowledge the man as he stepped up to the imprisoned female. He placed a hand on her chest, examining her. The ancient deity looked at one of the men and coldly remarked, "Since you enjoy causing pain and suffering with your primitive chemicals, then it's only fitting for you to endure it."

Streams of grayish blood shot out of the female and into the scientist. One of the men barely was able to scream as the substance went forcefully down his throat. He collapsed to the floor, his body contorting and spasming before finally dying. The scientists flipped the table so that it sat down horizontally and unshackled her wrists and ankles.

"You gnats have little time left to live. What were you doing to her?" the ancient deity asked, feeling bored, but wanted these men to squirm. Before they could answer, Harbinger coldly threatened, "If you say that it's classified, then I *will* kill you in a more colorful way than your colleagues on the floor."

"We're attempting to harness the different entities' natural abilities to create super soldiers, in theory," the man said as he rubbed the back of his neck. The woman shook her head and laughed to herself.

"Do you find this amusing, Dr. Arnica?" Harbinger turned his back, his gaze fell on her as he worked on the silent prisoner.

"Yes, I do. So much hubris in this place and within the higher-ups," the doctor said, waving her hand at the woman on the table. "I was sent here for both my extensive medical knowledge and alternative medicine. I get here and they have me playing mad scientist with all of these *creatures!* All I can do is treat them and tend to the many wounds that *we* inflict upon them! If you're going to kill us, then take me next. I can't do this anymore. I've been *this* close to going to the press just so I can be silenced forever."

Before the ancient deity could speak, the female on the table weakly spoke, "She speaks the truth. She's not right for this place. She deserves to be with us, not them."

Dr. Arnica stepped forward, her mouth gaping open as she saw the prisoner's wounds fully mending. Tears trickled down the doctor's face as she squeezed the woman's hand. "Gaylish, you don't mean that. Let this being end *my* suffering. You, of all your people, know that—"

Gaylish interrupted her as she sat up. "I know that you deserve to be with us. Of everyone here, you stood up to these pricks on numerous occasions, risking your life for our kind when no other person would. I'm surprised that you've not been shot yet,"

Dr. Arnica took off her lab coat and draped it over her back. The green-haired female pointed to her forearm and asked, "Harbinger, can you disable the implant they put in me? It cuts me off from my magic."

"Fucking bleeding-heart cunt," the scientist sneered as he spat on the floor. The worker swung a backhand towards the doctor, causing her to flinch, but he froze. Harbinger snapped his fingers and the two remaining scientists' necks broke in tandem. He grabbed Gaylish by her arm, and with a wave of his finger the device harmlessly dissolved.

Dr. Arnica cupped her hands over her mouth and dropped to her knees. She looked up at the ancient deity as he towered over her and asked, "Why did you do that? Why not me?"

Harbinger put his hand on her head. She wasn't sure what the deity was doing to her. Her head felt light and all of her synapses were firing at once. "Are you melting my brain?" Dr. Arnica bit out, not daring to move. "Is this my punishment?"

"No, healer," the ancient deity said. "I'm examining your mind to see what I need to see. I can't simply take their words for it, including your own. I can melt your brain, if that's your wish, but you are needed. Just not here."

"Are they going to get through the door, Harbinger?" Jacob asked as he focused solely on the only exit from the room.

"You're the seer," the ancient deity chuckled. "You tell me."

Dr. Arnica felt a sense of calm as the deity took his hand away. Gaylish held out her hand and helped the doctor to her feet. She looked at Harbinger and asked, "Did she pass? Will she be coming with us?"

"The doctor's alive, isn't she? I also slowed and reversed her aging, because she will need her youth when the time comes," the ancient deity replied with a shrug. Jasmine flew into the room, startling Dr. Arnica.

She looked at the ghost and asked, "Jasmine? What happened to you? Why are you—"

"She's with me now, and it was her choice and that's all you need to know at this point, healer," Harbinger harshly cut her off.

"*There's a dozen soldiers just outside the door...* " Jasmine said to the ancient deity. "*The other exam rooms are, in a sense, empty...*"

"Okay, but what does that mean?" Jacob asked, feeling confused.

"It means that the occupants that were in there for "treatment" are dead and haven't been disposed of yet," Gaylish answered as she eyed the ghost. She solemnly nodded as Harbinger walked over to the door.

He closed his eyes and stood at the door, listening to a thumping sound. The banging on the door had ceased and with a smirk he instructed, "Then take us to the holding cells. We have much work to do."

The ancient deity opened the door and stepped over the prone bodies of the soldiers. The men weren't dead, but seemed to be in a stupor. The flashing red lights created an eerie ambient lighting in the small corridor.

"I'm surprised you didn't just kill them," Jacob said as he lightly stepped over the downed soldiers.

"They will die when it's time. I wish that I could simply bring this structure down, but that would go against my plan," the ancient deity said as he pointed at the door. "Open it, seer."

"I wish that you would do it," Gaylish grumbled as the maintenance man swiped his red card over the electronic lock. "You don't know what I've witnessed here. These people—"

"Have done many cruel acts, but they're a necessary evil that is needed," Harbinger stated as he walked through the door, focusing on the magical trail that led to the prison cells.

He glanced at her and added, "I've seen in the minds of the different people here. Vile creatures that are way worse than the darkest of entities."

They walked down a long-sloped incline, the aroma of piss, vomit, and feces permeating the stagnant air. Along the far wall on the left was a makeshift jail, stretching the entire length of the room. Entities from different races and dimensions were packed within the lengthy cage, with little room and no privacy.

The creatures inside snarled, yelled profanities, and assaulted the bars; the creatures attacking the magically imbued bars received burns or simply got repelled from it. One demon pointed at the doctor and demanded, "Give us the bitch! We will teach her the meaning of pain!"

The ancient deity looked at the demon like it did at the humans that ran the facility, with contempt and boredom. "She's leaving this place with everyone else."

"Not before we have some fun with her first," the demon replied, and then noticed the ghost and chuckled. "Looks like the witch got what she rightfully deserved."

"Be silent, demon," Gaylish admonished. "These people are under his protection. I suggest that you hold your tongue or —"

"Or what? The big bad *destroyer of worlds* will kill me? I don't fear him or his power! He can free us all, but we all know that he won't be around to prevent us from taking our revenge! I will— Ahhhh!"

The demon cried out as all of his flesh was peeled off his body in one fluid motion of Harbinger's hand. The dark entity stood there in complete silence as shock took hold. The ancient deity grabbed the cell door and effortlessly ripped it off, flinging it across the room.

When Harbinger stepped inside all of the other entities, with the exception of the flayed demon, squeezed in uncomfortably tighter, not wanting to anger him in any way. He got in the demon's face and coldly ordered, "Go sit in the corner and consume yourself. Don't stop until there's nothing left, and don't forget your skin!"

The demon's eyes glazed over as he bent over and gathered his flayed skin and bundled it in his arms like it was a jumpsuit and stepped out of the cell. Harbinger glared at the other prisoners and intoned, "Anyone else that wishes to test my patience step forward now, otherwise, be silent and let me tell you what's going to happen next."

When none spoke up, the ancient deity motioned for the ones that followed him down here to join the others. Harbinger looked at everyone, gauging if anyone was going to make a move against the doctor or the maintenance guy.

Satisfied, he said, "I'm going to free all of you, but there's a price and a choice to be made. If it has escaped your notice, this world is becoming more and more reliant on technology. So much so that the humans don't bother taking care of nature or tending to it as they should. Besides Gaylish, does anyone know what must happen?"

All were silent, but a small green creature stepped forward. It was probably two and a half feet tall and had wrinkly green skin and no hair anywhere. His hands and feet had four digits with marble white claws at the ends. The tiny creature said, "The time for yet another Reset is upon us?"

"Correct, Adoy," Harbinger said calmly. The other entities were murmuring amongst themselves, trying to understand what the little creature spoke of as the ancient deity continued to speak. "When the balance between nature and civilization is skewed more towards technology, a Reset *must* occur. As some of you know this has occurred throughout the history of this world, just in small pockets. Now, all of humanity is becoming more connected to each other by technological means. It has been foreseen that nature will fall prey to individuals who prefer money over helping their environment and that humans become oblivious to it. This Reset will be a global cleansing. One that I'm overseeing."

"Are you going to wipe everyone off the face of the Earth?" Jacob asked as he looked nervously around the cell at the others.

"Use your ability and tell me what you see," the ancient deity replied.

He was about to argue when he stood rigid, his eyes turning white. "People are dying with blissful smiles. People are savagely killing others. A terrible sickness is causing all this madness. Supernatural creatures fighting side by side with humans in a war between good and evil..."

"Normally, when a Reset occurs all traces of the offending civilization are wiped out in the hopes that no one follows in their path to destruction. Since this is encompassing the entire world, I'm on the fence if I should destroy everything. Humanity will fall under three categories: Blissful Victims, The Ferals, and the Immune. The Immune are the ones who will be charged with the task of caring for nature after the Reset is finished, such as Dr. Arnica and Jacob here, because they have supernatural abilities. The rest of humanity will die either by their own hand or go crazy, killing indiscriminately."

"What does that have to do with us?" a gremlin asked. "If humanity is getting exterminated, then why give us a choice? Why do we have to pay a price for their stupidity?"

Gaylish turned around and addressed the little fae being. "The choice is simple, Hugo: Stay and help those Immune to the Reset or leave this world. As for the price," she looked at the ancient deity and said, "Harbinger can say what that will be."

The ancient deity waited for a moment before speaking, the sounds of human voices echoing not far away. "The price is part of participation. If you choose to aid humanity, there's a greater chance that many of you will find what you've been searching for your entire life. A life-mate. The veil on this world is already wavering. And by the time the Reset happens it *will* fall completely, making it easier to enter this world. You're physically here because of the rift that was torn in the veil by the meddling humans here. During the Reset, all that aren't normally seen *will* become corporeal. As the Reset draws nearer, you'll *all* hear the warning and can choose which side you'll be on. Good or evil, I don't care, but you will have to choose."

"And if we refuse to help?" Hugo cautiously asked.

"No life-mate. You can retreat to your own realms if you wish, but know that you will be squandering the chance to be complete. The Immunes are special for many reasons, so choose wisely, gremlin," Harbinger replied, then turned his head to look back at the way that they came in.

More chatter broke out as a large group of soldiers rushed down the inclined ramp, weapons drawn. The men aimed their weapons as the general strolled down the ramp, his cigar smoke trailing him like a locomotive smoke stack. He glared at the ancient deity and barked, "That's far enough, you filth! Come out of there and release your hostages!"

Harbinger coldly chuckled, "Good to see that you're finally up and about once again, Sergei. There are no hostages in here with me, only *your* prisoners."

"I see one of my maintenance men and Dr. Arnica in there, you fiend. Release them at once!" the general ordered.

"I can't, because they came with me willingly," the ancient deity replied with little emotion.

Perplexed, Sergei asked, "Why would anyone want to side with you, *monster?*"

Harbinger slowly smiled, causing the soldiers to feel unease and a sense of dread. "The reason is, as you *loved* to say, classified. Don't fret, General. We'll all be leaving shortly."

"The *hell* you are!" Sergei bellowed loudly. "Open fire! Kill the deity!"

The soldiers fired upon the ancient deity, yet he seemed unfazed. All the bullets that hit him simply bounced off and harmlessly fell on the concrete floor. Harbinger placed an energy field around all the occupants of the cell, keeping them safe. He opened a rift in the veil and a portal and said, "Those who don't want to be here, go through the rift. Whether you want to fight or not, spread the word of what's coming to this world. Those who wish to stay on Earth, enter the portal. It will close once everyone goes through it."

"Where will we end up?" Gaylish asked.

"Portland, Oregon," Jacob replied, his eyes white once again, "All we need will be there..."

Harbinger grunted in agreement as the entities fled. Dr. Arnica paused and anxiously said, "They *will* find us and —"

"*Let Harbinger deal with it...*" Jasmine cut her off, urging the doctor to step through the portal. The ancient deity finally turned his full attention to the soldiers attacking him. He put his hand up and all their weapons crumbled to dust. With a flick of his wrist all the soldiers, except for the general, dropped down on the floor, writhing in pain.

Harbinger aimed his hand at Sergei and forced the general to come to him. Harbinger grabbed him roughly by his throat, hoisting the general off the floor.

The ancient deity pulled the cigar out of Sergei's mouth and pressed the lit end against the man's forehead as he threatened, "Because of your arrogance, you and those you serve in the shadows *will* succumb to the horrors that you're creating here at this facility! Let this burn be a constant reminder! Everyone here will forget about Jacob and Dr. Arnica, but you *will* remember *me!*"

The god dropped the general, causing him to writhe in pain with his men. Harbinger turned on his heel and closed the rift as the last of the entities went through. Harbinger tweaked the portal so that it would take Gaylish and her small band of entities to Portland. Dr. Arnica asked the ancient deity, "What do we do when we go through this thing?"

With Jasmine hovering beside him, Harbinger coldly uttered as they both vanished together, "Prepare... The Reset *is* coming..."

A Bully's Comeuppance

Becky Threefeathers sighed as she closed her locker door. She rested her forehead against the cold metal, wishing that the final bell would ring so that her day would come to an end. Tears trickled down her cheeks, her breathing increasing with each passing moment. She wiped her face dry and pushed her long double braids over her shoulders and then opened her locker. She grabbed a notebook and her math book and sighed as she closed the locker door.

Why does high school have to be a living hell?

Every day, it was the same routine: rushing from class to class, tons of homework assignments, and getting picked on and made fun of by Doug Armstrong and his buddies. No matter what period it was, he managed to find her and make Becky's life miserable.

Becky got almost all of her clothes at the local thrift shops because her family was poor and Doug tended to find ways of ruining her clothes. She never knew what the prick would do next. Lately, he was making fun of her, calling her a *wetback* because of her complexion.

She told him that she was Cherokee many times, but it always fell on deaf ears. Doug Armstrong came from a wealthy family. He had no problems getting whatever he truly wanted, whether it was the latest trendy clothing or a top of the line sports car. Many of the girls fawned over him with the hopes that he would take notice of them and have a chance to be in his arms.

Doug could do no wrong, and the money that his family generously gave to the school caused the faculty to turn a blind eye. Becky tried filing complaints against him with the police, but somehow the team of family lawyers made it go away. Doug Armstrong was the epitome of privilege, and he knew it.

He has everything. Why must he focus on me?

Becky resigned herself to the fact that she was just another toy for Doug to play with, not caring how he made her feel. The guy went through girlfriends as fast as a roll of toilet paper during a bad bout of diarrhea. Becky couldn't understand why anyone in their right mind would want to have anything to do with the prick.

The first week after arriving at the new school, Doug asked Becky to be his girlfriend. He claimed that her beauty caused his heart to skip a beat and that meant, in his own words, that she was *the one*. Becky saw through his charm and false sincerity, having overheard him making the same claim to three other girls before then, and promptly turned him down. It was the next day that Doug revealed his true colors by calling her derogatory names and spreading rumors about her, and the relentless physical torture started.

That was five years ago.

The Cherokee girl had contemplated suicide on numerous occasions, just to escape her daily torment, but something always seemed to hold her back from actually doing it.

The bustle of the other students around her made it difficult to get to class. As Becky left the main building to walk over to the newer Armstrong Annex the rain let up, which caused her to smile. She walked briskly, but her smile faded when she saw Doug standing by the glass doors, making out with Missy Walker, his latest girlfriend. She was about 6'2", barely taller than Doug, wavy blonde hair, ample breasts, and played on the high school basketball team.

What torture will he inflict on me today?

He glanced over at Becky as his hands snaked into the inside of Missy's pants, fondling her ass. The Cherokee ignored him with disgust as she tried to get by them, but Doug blocked her way into the building.

"Where's my favorite little *wetback* going in such a rush?" Doug asked as he pulled his tongue out of Missy's mouth.

"To class, obviously. Now, if you two will excuse me," Becky replied curtly, trying to grab the door handle. Missy grabbed Becky by one of her braids, causing her to yelp, and yanked her back as Doug untangled himself from her.

"That's quite rude of you, don't you think, Doug?" Missy snidely asked, looking down at the Cherokee.

"Indeed. You should know your place, little *wetback*. One call to immigration and I'll have you and your whole family deported," Doug smugly remarked.

"Save your breath," Becky retorted, "I'm Native American and I was born here. If anyone needs deporting, it's dimwitted, shortsighted buffoons like yourself!"

"Everyone knows that Native Americans were nothing more than Mexicans that infested these lands like a terrible plague," Doug replied as he grabbed Becky roughly by her arm, dragging her to the other side of the building, away from prying eyes. "My father's supplying this school with the new history textbooks that tell all about this fact. Do you know why?"

"Because he's rich, white, and doesn't want the newer generations to know that the greatest genocide happened on American soil? Colonizers have been trying to wipe my people out for centuries, so why not do the same in the history books?" Becky snarked.

Missy walked up to the Cherokee, knocking her math book out of her hands, and then slapped her face, "Oh, shut up and get over it! Boohoo, your people got slaughtered. Just because we're white, it is not our damn fault. We weren't the ones that pulled the trigger. That happened hundreds of years ago."

"And yet his father is *still* fanning the flames to burn all knowledge of the genocide away with those doctored textbooks. Hundreds of years may have passed, but nothing has changed," Becky replied as she rubbed her cheek.

"I suppose that it's my fault that I'm white, isn't it?" Doug said with a sneer. "I'm proud of my family and the wealth we accumulated over the years. Something that you'll never have within your grasp."

"You're right." The Cherokee grinned. "Which is why I turned you down years ago. Face it, Missy, you'll be his arm candy for a short while and then he'll move on to the next desperate piece of ass, like a locust. You're just this week's flavor."

"Hold her, Doug!" Missy angrily hissed. He grabbed Becky, holding her with her arms bent behind her back. Becky kicked at Missy, but she dodged them with ease. "I believe it's high time that you were taught a lesson. I have the perfect one in mind for you, *wetback*!"

Becky snarled, "I'm not a— OOPH," the Cherokee got cut off as the basketball player punched her in the gut. Missy smiled as she reared back and landed another gut punch. After several more blows Becky was wheezing and crying, much to Doug's delight.

"Do you have your pocket knife on you, sweetheart?" Missy asked with a glint of malice in her eyes. Doug squeezed Becky's arms painfully together, holding them in place with one arm as he rummaged in his jeans pocket.

"As luck would have it, I do," Doug jovially announced as he handed it to his girlfriend. "What are you going to do with it?"

Missy snapped the blade out, wiggling it so that the sunlight glinted on it. "I'm taking a few souvenirs from our girl here."

She roughly grabbed both of Becky's braids, holding them taut. The Cherokee tried to free herself from Doug, but he held her tightly as his girlfriend cut each of her braids off.

"No! You fucking bitch!" Becky bit out between her sobs. Missy shook both of the braids triumphantly in the Cherokee's face and coldly remarked, "I'm not done collecting from you. Doug, bend this little skank over, but have her facing you."

"With pleasure." Doug grinned as he twisted the Cherokee around, bending her so that all Becky could see was his legs and shoes. She felt the back of her sweatshirt being lifted up by Doug's girlfriend and then something cold touching her bare skin by her bra.

"Stop it," Becky pleaded as she felt her bra getting cut off at the straps and then it was unhooked and yanked free. Missy ordered,

"Move over to your left, dear. I have one more idea."

Doug shuffled her over a few feet, smiling brightly, knowing exactly what Missy was planning to do. Becky gasped when she felt her leggings get yanked down to her ankles. The Cherokee silently cried, praying that these two would finish up and leave her alone.

Missy tsked as she put a hand on Becky's hip. "Sheesh, can't you afford any designer clothes? No matter. At least it won't be a total loss."

Doug's girlfriend grabbed the fabric of Becky's panties and, using the pocket knife, cut them off on both sides. Doug eyed his girlfriend as he stepped to the side, still holding the Cherokee. Missy kicked Becky's bare ass with the sole of her shoe as Doug released her, sending her tumbling forward into a puddle of mud.

Becky could hear the sound of footsteps next to her as she heard Doug say with delight, "Thanks for the undergarments, Becky. I'm going to use them as proof to the entire student body that you finally relented to my charms and had sex with me. I'm going to tell them that you love it rough, hence why your bra and panties are torn. I hope you enjoy your new reputation as the *wetback* slut."

They were laughing so loudly that it caught the attention of one of the teachers. He cried out with concern, "Hey! What's going on here?"

"Sorry, Mr. Taylor," Missy said as she discreetly hid Becky's braids in her pocket and she pointed at the Cherokee. "We saw poor Becky stumble and fall. We came to help, but—"

"Why are her pants down at her ankles?" The teacher asked, his gaze suspiciously on Doug.

"How should I know? It's not my fault that she had an *obvious* wardrobe malfunction. I believe that her hand-me-down clothing finally failed and this is the end result. Isn't that what happened, Becky?" Doug said with his best fake sincere look of innocence.

Mr. Taylor looked down at the Cherokee as she slowly pushed herself out of the mud puddle, to her knees. She tugged down her sweatshirt and sighed, "They speak the truth. The elastic gave way in my leggings, which caused me to...trip and fall."

Becky crawled out of the mud and managed to get to her feet. With shaky hands, she tugged her soiled leggings up as Doug and his girlfriend giggled. Mr. Taylor glared at them and said, "Enough of that. The show's over, now get to class. Both of you."

As they left, still laughing, Missy shouted, "Next time wear a belt, Becky, so everyone won't see your ass!"

The Cherokee slowly walked over and picked up her math book off the wet grass. She closed her eyes, wishing that there was something that she could do to stop Doug's bullying. He had humiliated her numerous times, but this was the first time that she had been violated. It may have been Missy assaulting her, but the Cherokee knew that Doug had planned it out.

Becky flinched when she felt a hand touch her elbow. She looked over at Mr. Taylor as he asked, "Tell me what *really* happened, Becky."

She shrugged her shoulders. "It happened like I said. There's nothing that can be done about it."

"I've heard that Doug's been bullying you for a while now," the teacher said, trying to get her to speak up. "Just say what really occurred and I'll see to it that he's held accountable for his actions."

Becky couldn't look at him. She stared vacantly at the mud puddle and muttered, "You don't get it. None of you do. There's nothing that can be done. May I be excused so that I can go home and change clothes?"

Mr. Taylor nodded and asked, "Shall we go to the office and call your parents to come get you?"

Becky slowly walked away, shaking her head as thunder rumbled in the dark sky. "No, they're both at work. My house isn't that far from here. I can walk."

"You sure?"

Becky paused, more tears trickling down her mud-caked face. "Yes. I need some alone time and the walk will help."

As if on cue, the rain came down hard as Becky walked down the gravel road. She didn't care that she was getting drenched.

At least the rain will wash most of the mud away.

The Cherokee held her textbook against her stomach, wincing from the beating she had received. A part of Becky had wished that Missy would have slit her throat and put an end to her suffering. The path leading to her home was shrouded by a large forest on both sides as the Cherokee trudged down it.

Her thoughts were getting darker by the second and then someone spoke.

"Becky..."

The Cherokee paused, wondering if she was hearing things or simply the rain making strange sounds around her. She shook her head and kept on walking.

"Becky Threefeathers..."

Becky froze on the path, the slick little hairs on the back of her neck standing up. She turned and looked in the direction of where she believed the voice came from. Before her, standing next to a rotting felled tree, was a seven-foot- tall creature with disproportionately long arms and legs. Becky couldn't see its actual face because it was wearing the skull of buck; its antlers had bits of mud and moss caked to it.

Becky walked up to the creature and dropped down to her knees before it and said, "I know what you are. Do me a favor and kill me quickly. It's what I want."

The creature towered over the Cherokee with its head cocked to the side. It reached out one of its gangly arms and took one of the stubs from what was left of her braid in its fingers and said, *"I don't want to kill you, Becky Threefeathers. Though I am hungry, you'll not be in my belly."*

Becky laughed hysterically. "I'm not even worth a Wendigo's hunger. I suppose that is to be expected. My life is nothing but pain and suffering."

"We both needlessly suffer. The only difference between us is that you can end yours. I need my hunger to be sated."

"I offer myself to you freely," Becky said, looking up at the Wendigo. "Take me and end both of our suffering."

The creature slowly walked around the Cherokee, its bare feet making little sound. *"It does please me that you would be so generous, but I must decline the offer."*

Confused, the Cherokee asked, "What is it that you want from me?"

The supernatural creature replied, *"I've been watching over you for a while now. Seeing the suffering that you endure has made me grow fond of you, which is why I don't want to eat you. I have a little proposal for you; if you'll listen and stop trying to get me to kill you, I'll tell you."*

Becky huffed as she stood up. "Fine. Speak your piece fast before I catch pneumonia."

The Wendigo chuckled. "*You won't like it, but I can guarantee that you won't be tormented any more if you let me…possess you.*"

The Cherokee nervously bit her bottom lip. "Will this hurt?"

"*No, but I will make sure that we both get what we need,*" the creature honestly said as it stood in front of her. It leaned forward, getting near Becky's dirty face. "*The plan is simple and fool-proof. Do you trust me, Becky Threefeathers?*"

"No, but what choice do I have? Tell me your plan," Becky said as she let her shoulders slump in defeat.

"*Wise girl. First, get cleaned up and rest,*" the Wendigo stated as it stood back up. The creature reached out and tenderly caressed her cheek. "*I'll reveal all shortly.*"

Becky smiled slightly as she walked over to the path, heading to her home.

The next day Becky entered the school wearing blue jeans, hiking boots, and a white cotton t-shirt. She could hear the other kids snickering and whispering as she walked by. Becky had a feeling that Doug and Missy had spread the rumor already, probably through social media, but she didn't care.

The one thing that she wanted to do was to find Doug. Nothing else mattered. A couple of guys walked beside her and handed her paper with their phone numbers on it, saying that they were available anytime. Girls sneered and glared at the Cherokee, gossiping amongst themselves.

What little was left of her hair Becky managed to fix up nicely, accenting it with a wreath woven from the vine cordage from the forest. She spotted Doug standing by his locker, boasting and making obscene sexual gestures with several of his buddies next to him.

He glanced over and saw Becky moving towards him, which caused him to pause for a moment, but then he jovially announced, "There's my little freak now! You forgot your undergarments at my house last night. Would you like them back?"

Becky slowed her movement as she approached him, her face twisted with a predatory smile as she eyed Doug possessively. Doug wasn't sure what to expect from her, but his throat felt parched. Becky never looked at him this way before.

The Cherokee noticed as Doug's leering buddies moved out of her way, Missy was coming around the corner. Becky got in Doug's face, pressing her lips against his as she grabbed him by his crotch. As the guys cheered and whistled, Becky breathlessly whispered with a possessive growl, "Keep them. I know that you want them as much as you want me."

Doug's eyes glassed over as he stood there, his lips parted in shock. Missy stormed over, her fists balled up as she screeched, "Get your filthy hands off of *my man*, you nasty little slut!"

Becky backed away with a knowing smirk. "Don't act like you don't know about it. *You* were there, too. Everyone is talking about *us* today."

Missy's face flushed with anger as she draped herself on Doug. As his friends gasped in surprise and laughed, he grabbed Missy and pressed her firmly against the lockers. She smiled at him, but noticed the strange vacant look now took on more of a predatory gaze. Missy was about to speak when Doug repeatedly punched her in the face, bloodying her nose and mouth.

Missy skidded down the lockers, stunned as tears trickled down her swollen face. Doug turned around to his buddies, glaring as he grabbed the nearest one and bit down on the guy's arm. He screamed, trying to get Doug off of him. "Fuck! What are you doing!"

Doug yanked his head back, ripping a chunk of muscle away. As he slowly chewed it, everyone backed away as he hungrily eyed them like a ravenous beast. Becky skirted by him without getting bit and kneeled down by Missy. As she assisted the unsteady girl to her feet, the Cherokee draped her arm around her and whispered gently, "Come along with me. I know where you need to go."

Becky walked out of the building as Doug went on a violent rampage. Anyone who came near him got chunks of flesh and muscle torn off. All the while, Doug kept repeating the same thing in a guttural growl, "I'm hungry!"

A girl barely stepped out of the bathroom and was yanked into his arms. Doug bit a chunk of flesh out of her shoulder before she had time to scream. He let the girl drop at his feet as he charged at one of the football players. The athlete had a fire extinguisher in his beefy hands, wielding it like a club.

He swung it several times at his head, but missed. Doug easily dodged the assault and then, when the opportunity presented itself, he jumped onto the football player, tackling him to the floor. He knocked the fire extinguisher away and snatched up the guy's hand and bit off three of his fingers.

Doug stood up as several teachers rushed into the hall, trying to sequester the chaotic student body into various classrooms. The principal looked at Doug in shock, seeing the blood running down his chin as he chewed off his own lips.

"D-Doug?" the principal stammered as he held up his hands, looking for a place to hide. "Doug Armstrong, what's gotten into you?"

"I'm hungry!" Doug bellowed as he punched the principal in the face, knocking him out. He stood over his latest victim, but then he looked up at the ceiling. He grinned menacingly at the camera before bolting from the school.

The bully ran down the road, still muttering about being hungry as sirens and flashing red and blue lights filled the area. He moved swiftly, heading into the forest like a wild animal on the hunt, sniffing out his next prey.

Becky quietly stood next to Missy as the basketball player looked around at her surroundings. Through bleary eyes, the basketball player could tell that she wasn't at the school infirmary. It smelled damp and musty, and everything around her was dark. Despite her concussion, Missy knew that something was off as her entire body shivered from the cold.

"Where am I?" Missy asked.

She tried to get up but, to her horror, she was tied down to a plastic table. Missy yanked at her bindings, but they held her in place. She flinched when she felt hands slipping into her jean pockets, so she cried out, "Who are you and why are you doing this to me?"

"Shhhh," Becky said as she pulled out not only her braids but Doug's pocket knife as well. "Doug Armstrong will be here soon to take care of you."

Fear laced her shrill voice as she shrieked, "No! Keep that bastard away from me! Whoever you are, please let me go!"

"Why should I?" Becky let the ambient light from her cell phone light up her visage. The Cherokee sneered as she added, "You two are meant for each other. Don't worry, this *slut* wouldn't dream of coming between you and your one true love."

"Becky!" Missy bit out in surprise. "Why are you doing this?" She heard the unmistakable click of Doug's pocket knife being opened and, full of panic, she cried out, "Please don't hurt me! I'm sorry about yesterday! I'll never hurt you again! I promise!"

"This I know," the Cherokee coldly remarked as she grabbed Missy's shirt and slowly cut the fabric apart. "Just know that you brought this upon yourself, Missy. You attacked me, so by right as a Cherokee I get to exact my revenge."

"Please no!" the basketball player pleaded, tears streaming down her bloody face. "If you want Doug, you can have him! Don't —"

Becky slapped her prisoner hard across her face just as the fabric from her shirt fell open. She leaned in next to Missy's ear and whispered, "You think that this is all about *him*? You're a damn fool. I'm going to take my own souvenirs from you, and then you'll be ready for Doug when he arrives."

Missy felt the cold steel of the blade against her skin as Becky cut the straps off of her bra. She tugged and pulled it from Missy with ease. The prisoner squirmed and bucked her hips when she felt the Cherokee unbuttoning her jeans. Becky laughed as she pulled down Missy's jeans, making sure that they were at the girl's ankles.

"These are *mine,*" the Cherokee growled as she forcefully ripped off Missy's lace panties with ease, causing her to yelp. Becky put the sharp edge of the blade against her prisoner's heart and slowly carved an intricate symbol into her sweaty flesh. Missy screamed loudly, her sobbing echoing throughout the room.

As Becky finished she heard a low, guttural growl behind her. She smiled as she looked at Doug, who was sweating and breathing heavily. She walked over to him and put a hand on his chest. "See, Missy? I told you that Doug would come for you. I can tell from his expression that he wants you badly."

"Keep that prick away from me!" Missy cried. She was going to say more, but she froze with fear when Becky turned on a small camping lantern, revealing that they were in some sort of cave. She saw Doug's eyes glowing red, his face appearing as though it had sunken in. She could have sworn that he had razor-sharp teeth and his sweet lips were gone as his jaw chattered repeatedly together, "I'm hungry!"

Becky tucked her souvenirs into her pockets, wiped her fingerprints off the pocket knife, and put it in Doug's hand as she said, "I can tell that you are. I've prepared and made her ready for you. *Bon appetit*, my friend."

Missy cried out to Becky as she walked away, but then pleaded to Doug as he advanced towards her. The Cherokee smiled as she heard the first of Missy's screams echoing in the cave.

A phone call from Becky told the police that she had seen Doug Armstrong going into a nearby cave on her property. When the police entered the cave, they found Doug consuming the lifeless corpse of Missy Walker. He didn't put up a struggle, but kept saying that he didn't know how he had gotten there.

When asked why he did what he did, all Doug Armstrong could say was that he was hungry and had no control. He also claimed that he was watching everything that he did, but couldn't do anything to stop himself.

As the police slowly drove off with him in the back of the squad car, Doug saw Becky standing on the side of the path to her house.

She waved mockingly and blew Doug a kiss as a tall, gangly creature with a buck skull stood behind her.

Becky thought to herself, *All of your family's fortune won't be able to save your ass this time, Doug Armstrong!*

A Watery Grave

"No, you can't do this!" Mary protested as the sailors grabbed her by her arms, while two other men came up beside her with a thick rope, binding her hands. "You can't be serious!"

The captain chuckled as he pointed out, "I'm sorry, milady, but my hands are tied in this matter. Just like yours are about to be."

"I-I'm *not* a lady, Captain Brady," Mary pleaded.

"Is that a fact?" the captain replied as he pointed to one of his men. "Pete there saw you while you were getting undressed. He claims otherwise."

"Pete never liked me in the first place," Mary growled as she spit in her accuser's direction. "He'd say anything to get me thrown off your ship."

"Be that as it may," Captain Brady said as he got mere inches from Mary's face with a knowing stare, "we both know that there's one sure fire way to find out who's being honest, don't we, *Mark*?"

Mary gulped as the captain grabbed the hem of her trousers and her underwear and, with one fluid movement, yanked them down to her ankles. Several of the sailors gasped as she looked away in shame. Pete smugly grinned as the captain looked at her crotch.

"Either you're a eunuch or a woman. From what I can see, I'm leaning towards the latter. Tie *Mark* up, boys. It's time to change our fortune."

Mary grunted as the ropes got tighter, the tiny fibers stinging her skin like a swarm of bees. She squirmed as the men lashed her legs together, pulling her trousers and underwear off completely.

"Seriously? You're going to toss me over the side, just because you guys are having a little bad luck on this voyage?" Mary shouted incredulously.

The old schooner bounced and swayed in the rough, choppy waters. The storm clouds overhead promised a heavy downpour as lightning streaked throughout the dark sky. For days, the fishermen's nets were coming up empty. In a few instances, a few of the nets were lost or had been torn apart.

The men of *The Privateer* were growing restless and irritated, looking for something or someone to blame, because when there's no catch they didn't get paid. Every occurrence made the sailors more paranoid and seeking a means to end this streak of bad luck, especially Pete.

There were only a few new deckhands on this voyage and Pete wondered if one of the greenhorns had something to do with it. He snuck around and silently observed each one. *Mark* seemed to be the one who was the most peculiar of them all. *Mark* barely understood orders that were given and didn't know the different terminology that most fishermen knew.

Even the man's face appeared fairer than most; his hands were too dainty and barely had any calluses on them, despite claiming to come from a family of fishermen. They argued over many subjects and, on more than one occasion, Pete could have sworn that *Mark's* voice changed, sounding more feminine.

Unbeknownst to the crew, including Captain Brady, Pete had created small spy holes throughout the entire ship. His efforts were being rewarded today as he watched *Mark* undress while the other sailors slept in their hammocks. The sailor informed the captain about the woman, insisting that she was the reason for all of their burdens on this voyage.

The sailors dragged Mary to the port side and bent her over the railing. She felt a hand smack her bare ass and said, "It would be a shame to throw this fine piece of ass overboard before dipping into her slick cargo hold."

A cold chill ran through her body at the idea that these men would sexually molest her before killing her. Mary grunted, trying to topple herself into the water as several hands held her in place. She heard the unmistakable click of a flintlock hammer being cocked back and then Captain Brady barked out, "If you do, then you'll be joining her at the bottom of the sea. If anyone wants to fuck her, be my guest, but know that her bad luck will be upon you as well. Choose wisely, boys."

The men moved away from the bound female as the captain put his hand on her shoulder. "Nothing personal, but we can't afford no more bad luck. What is your name and why did you sneak onto my ship in the first place?"

"Why do you care about knowing my name?" Mary bitterly gulped as she stared down at the icy churning waters, resigned to the reality that it would be her grave. She could have sworn that she saw several large fish with strange fins that resembled arms keeping pace with the old schooner. "I'll be dead, and soon your nets shall be full of fat fish."

"I ask because I personally want a name and a reason why you would risk everything to be out here with us. I don't like killing, especially women, but if I don't do this you'll suffer a fate worse than the sea's embrace. Plus, when we make our way to port and people are searching for you, a husband or your father, I want them to know. It's not right for them to needlessly suffer."

"Mary. Mary Fairchild. I wanted to see the world and experience life at sea, you know. This was the only way that I could make it happen, because no one wants a woman on board. Don't worry, just forget about me. No one will be looking for me."

Captain Brady sighed. "I hate to do this to you, Mary, I truly do." She felt the tips of his fingers slightly caressing her back. "I wish that we had met under different circumstances. I can't imagine how a bonnie lass such as yourself wouldn't have a man or two scouring the countryside for you."

Mary felt the captain grab a hold of the ropes attached to her legs, preparing to toss her over, filling the pit of her stomach with dread. Several men, including Pete, cheered as Captain Brady solemnly said, "Give our regards to Davy Jones when you meet him. I'm truly sorry for doing this to you, Mary Fairchild."

Mary tumbled end over end, crashing into the salt water, the cold shock causing her to gasp and inhale water.

Pete grabbed the woman's clothes and tossed them overboard and proclaimed, "No more of her terrible luck shall vex us!"

As a deluge of rainfall soaked everyone, Captain Brady ordered the sailors to get back to work and prepare for the squall that was now upon them. In the dark recesses of his mind, the captain looked up at the storm as he made his way to the helm, wondering if murdering the poor woman was the right thing to do.

Mary plunged deeper into the ocean, wiggling and thrashing the whole way down. She could no longer make out the silhouette of the schooner. Her lungs were burning, demanding oxygen that wouldn't be coming any time soon.

Why not just shoot me and put me out of my suffering?

Her entire body felt like it was being crushed by an unseen vise. Mary kept seeing large fish darting around her as everything in the sea faded to black. She felt several pairs of hands grabbing her and then a sharp pain in her neck before her world went completely black.

Mary opened her eyes as pain coursed throughout her entire body. She let out a wail of agony, which sounded strange and disturbing. Mary grabbed at her throat. As she rubbed it, something didn't feel right. Her skin was smooth, but she noticed small ridges all over it.

What added to Mary's confusion was the sight of a shimmering school of mackerel swimming in front of her. She looked around at her surroundings and saw that she was still underwater, somehow alive and in a cavern.

How is this possible?

She cast her gaze at her own body and saw that she was no longer bound in ropes, and even her hands were free. Her legs resembled the tail of a huge fish. Mary cringed when she saw that her hands had translucent webbing between each finger, and her nails were now thick, blue claws.

Mary had no clothing left on her body, the garments she used to conceal her ample breasts nowhere to be found. She felt so bewildered by her situation that she didn't notice something touching her shoulder.

"I see that you're awake," a female voice said next to Mary's ear, causing her to roll down on the sandy seabed. She flopped around, having difficulty controlling her new form. Mary saw the woman swaying in the water effortlessly, smiling, revealing her razor-sharp teeth.

The mystery woman had a similar fish body as Mary. She was beautiful and terrifying at the same time. Mary was surprised that she could actually hear clearly as the female added, "I'm happy to see that your transformation was a success."

"W-Who," Mary stammered, trying to get the words out. "What are you?"

The fish woman glided down and helped Mary up as she replied, "We're sisters now, so it's my job to train you on how to use your new form."

"Where am I? What's happening to me?" Mary demanded as she attempted to crawl away backwards. The fish woman caught her by wrapping her arms under Mary's arms.

She effortlessly lifted her up and got inches from her face and said, "My people saw what those cruel men did to you. You were all tied up and slowly dying, land-dweller. This isn't the first time we've had to save a woman who's been cast down to the depths of our domain. You certainly won't be last."

Mary gulped, memories spilling into her mind like a dam that gave way to millions of gallons of water. "Why aren't I dead?"

"We changed you into one of us. Isn't that delightful?" the fish woman proudly answered. She hugged Mary tightly as she added, "Your people have different names for us. I'm sure that you know about *mermaids*?"

"This can't be happening," Mary replied. "That's not possible!"

"You say that and yet," the fish woman said as she let her go, waving her hand at her, "you are now one of us. That's why you can breathe down here and speak to me."

Mary gulped as she looked at the fish woman. She noticed that she had gills on the sides of her neck, so Mary reached up and touched her own neck. She felt the small flaps of skin moving in tandem with her breathing.

Movement just out of her peripheral caught Mary by surprise as more mermaids swam around her. She was mesmerized by how beautiful they were and how effortlessly they swam around her. They each had hand-fashioned weapons that resembled a spear that had been meshed with a sword. Mary attempted to swim, but ended up thrashing around like she caught on the end of a fisherman's hook.

She looked nervously at the others, expecting to be mocked for her failure, but it didn't happen. The mermaids circled her and grabbed her by her arms, holding her in place as another mermaid appeared before her.

"I take it she's our new sister, Coral?" One of the new mermaids asked, her crimson hair waving in the water like fire.

"Yes, Litha. She's just come to and I've not had a chance to teach her yet. She's still in shock," Coral replied as she bowed her head slightly.

"What's your name, land-dweller?" Litha asked with an air of authority.

"Mary. Mary Fairchild," the newly-transformed mermaid replied, bowing her head.

"Not anymore," Litha stated, "Mary Fairchild is dead and gone. You need a new name to go with your new form. The life you once knew ceases to exist. Water is your new way of life. As such, you must learn to swim and hunt like the rest of us or you will not last long. Understand?"

Mary nodded slowly and said, "Will you teach me?"

"Coral will, but first you must choose a name for yourself. Your training shall begin once you do this. It signifies your place in our pod," Litha explained.

Mary thought about her life on land and the short time on the schooner. Nothing but pain and sorrow was her way of life it seemed, so she said to the leader of the mermaids, "Just call me Quisling. It's all I know that fits."

Litha chuckled, "An appropriate name. One that *will* be an integral part of your new life. Coral, teach her the basics so we can teach her how to properly hunt."

"Of course, Litha," Coral replied. She turned to her new sister and said as the leader swam away, "Okay, *Quisling*. Watch what I do with my body and try to mimic what you see."

Quisling nodded as she observed Coral swaying her hips from side to side as the other mermaids held her arms to steady her. The new mermaid was a little jerky with her movements, but eventually Quisling got it to the point that her new sisters released her.

She smiled, but then the new mermaid clutched her stomach as violent cramping took hold. Coral saw the pain in Quisling's eyes and motioned to someone that the new mermaid couldn't see.

Another mermaid silently swam next to Quisling and held out a spear sword and said,

"This is yours. Keep it near you at all times, especially for tonight."

Quisling croaked out, "Why? What's happening tonight?"

"We're going on the hunt, sister," the other mermaid replied as Coral came over to her. She lashed a rope around Quisling and attached her new weapon to it.

She hugged the new mermaid and sympathetically whispered in her ear, "The pain you're feeling means that the transformation is nearly complete. It requires one last ingredient."

"What is it?" Quisling desperately asked, wanting the pain to subside. "If you have it, please give it to me!"

"Unfortunately I can't, but that's why we must hunt. If we don't, you *will* die from the pain. The last ingredient is the flesh of land-dwellers."

"How can I do that??" Quisling bit out. "I'm useless like this!"

"The pain will lessen when we get to dry land, but it won't fully go away. It's a reminder of what you have to do in order to survive. The pain is an indication that you must feed, but after tonight, if we're successful, it won't be this harsh. Your body will eat you alive, slowly digesting you from the inside out. Do you understand what I'm saying, sister?"

Quisling nodded. Even though the thought of killing someone seemed barbaric and wrong, her mind latched on to the idea to the point of it becoming an obsession. Maybe it was the pain causing her to think about it as a cure to her voracious agony, so the new mermaid settled on the notion that she had to do this or die.

"Good," Coral purred, sending a seductive feeling throughout Quisling's new body. "We have a plan and the perfect spot to hunt. Take my hand and I'll teach you what you need to do."

As *The Privateer* docked in the harbor, the sailors were all smiles and in great spirits. Their cargo hold was filled with an abundance of fish. Captain Brady oversaw the crew as the deckhands tied the ship to dock while workers from the dock assisted in unloading their catch.

Off in the distance on the beach, a small fire burned in the evening light. Songs from the women dancing around the fire carried in the wind, assailing not only his ears but the sailors' as well. Pete rushed into the cabin, grinning from ear to ear, and stated, "The ship's secured, captain. The men are requesting to take their leave and indulge in the local nightlife here."

Captain Brady curtly nodded, but warned, "Permission granted, but let them know that it will be all our necks if even one of them lets slip what we did to Mary at sea. Loose lips can sink us to the bottom, like she did."

Pete nodded. "Aye, Captain. I'll remind them all. See you out at the pub?"

"Maybe." Brady glanced back at the beach. "Lord knows I could use a stiff drink or twenty."

Pete followed his gaze and smirked. "I think that little party over there might be the best place for us all to unwind. I'm fairly certain that they'll be willing to entertain us on this night."

Captain Brady nodded. "You have a point. Don't get into too much trouble before I get there."

Pete replied with a chuckle as he stepped out of the cabin, "Wouldn't think of it. I'll try not to sully all of them before you arrive."

The captain shook his head in disgust, but never took his eyes off the campfire celebration. He wasn't sure why, but Brady felt an irresistible urge to leave the ship. The man was so caught up in the scene that he didn't hear a young man saying his name, "Captain? Captain Jack Brady?"

A tug on his sleeve caused him to jump. Captain Brady glared at the young man, but his ire lessened when he saw that the man was holding a thick book as he stood next to the harbormaster.

"My apologies, I didn't hear you come in," he stated nervously. "Yes , I'm Captain Brady."

"I'm James and this here is Griswold. I'm here to inform you that your cargo hold is empty. I just need your signature to sign off on the final count."

The captain took the book and scanned over it. He smiled, knowing that he and his crew were going to get paid handsomely for the day's catch. He signed it and handed it back to James, who said, "Thanks for your business. Come see me in my office this week to collect your money. Good night, Captain."

As James strolled out the harbormaster remained in place, causing Brady's stomach to sour.

This can't be good.

The portly older man slowly walked around the cabin, scratching his stubbled chin as he said, "I noticed that you're one man down on your roster from when you set sail. Mind telling me what happened out there, Captain?"

Brady gulped slightly, but decided to tell what sort of happened, "Mark Smith was lost to the sea. We ran into a harsh squall and he went overboard as everyone was trying to secure the equipment. His leg got tangled in one of the weighted net lines and down he went."

"I see," the harbormaster said, his wrinkled face remaining impassive as he stopped to observe the beach party. "Another tragedy at sea. It's a strange thing."

"Excuse me?"

Griswold pointed at the women. "Sorry. I'm referring to them. I've been around here for a long time and I've noticed a thing or two. An odd thing keeps occurring. Have you noticed it yet, Brady?"

The captain shrugged his shoulders, still unsure if the harbormaster suspected foul play. "No, I haven't. What does that party mean to you? I've never seen it here until now."

Griswold turned around and looked Captain Brady in his eyes and said, "Every time there's a tragedy that befalls a vessel coming into our port, *The Siren's Song* gathers on that secluded beach. Singing and dancing. A strange coincidence, which is why I wanted to know if you had lost someone or if the missing person was left at a different port. I'm superstitious to a fault and this is becoming more factual, in my opinion."

As the captain let out a pinned breath, Griswold put his hand on his shoulder. "Don't fret, lad. I didn't think that you did something terrible. I only ask the captains about this when I see the discrepancy on their manifest."

Brady replied rapidly, "I apologize for not updating it —"

Griswold cut off the troubled captain, "Don't worry. I could see that storm you ran through and expected the worst. Update it at your convenience."

Brady looked back at the beach party and asked, "*The Siren's Song,* you say?"

"Yes, Jack," the harbormaster said as he visibly shook like he had a cold chill. "Like I said, I'm superstitious, and with a name like that and how they seem to know when a tragedy hits is odd to say the least. Maybe I'm an old fool, but the village is fine with them doing what they do because it brings in more revenue to the other merchants. Don't rightly know how those women do it, but they do. Feel free to go join the party."

"Why not come along with me?" Captain Brady asked.

Griswold tipped his hat and shot him a wry grin as he walked out of the cabin. "It's a party of alcohol and debauchery. They don't have what I desire between those legs, if you catch my meaning, Captain."

Captain Brady nodded as he walked over to the port window. He picked up a pair of binoculars and looked at the dancing women. He found himself humming to the music that they were singing, despite being so far away. Each woman looked exotic, with perfect skin, and wore only the smiles on their unblemished visages.

Most of his crew were already joining the ladies; each man looked ecstatic and having a good time, drinking and groping the women.

Jack felt his mouth salivating until he saw one female in particular. At that moment all the lustful thoughts he had slipped away, his mouth becoming as arid as the desert.

It's her! Mary Fairchild!

Her eyes seemed to lock with his, despite the distance and lighting, as she swayed rhythmically to the music. She lifted her arm, beckoning him to join the party as she licked her lips and let her other hand seductively travel up and down her body.

Captain Brady dropped the binoculars on the cabin floor as his eyes glazed over, like he was in a trance, and uttered, "I'm coming, Miss Fairchild! Please forgive me!"

The women of *The Siren's Song* danced around the fire, singing songs that had no actual words. They watched as the crew of *The Privateer* disembarked, which was their cue to draw the sailors to them. It didn't take much effort for the mermaids to track down the schooner. Quisling told them exactly where the ship planned to make port.

The breezy night assisted in carrying their song to their intended prey. Coral told Quisling to stay in the background since these men knew what she looked like, but once the sailors were under their control the new mermaid could fully join in the merriment.

She conveyed that the one called Pete would be the one that she wanted to eat first, but also had a special plan for Captain Brady, if he came to the party. The sailors wandered up to the festive bonfire, their eyes fixed on the naked flesh as the mermaids circled around them. The humming intensified to the point that each man's eyes were glazed over and were in a hazy trance.

"You boys are overdressed for our welcoming party," Coral purred as she touched each man. "This is a skyclad party. No clothing allowed. Strip and let's enjoy each other's company tonight."

The sailors nodded in unison as they disrobed. Coral looked over and saw Quisling and said, "Is your final ingredient here, sister?"

"Yes," Quisling replied in disgust. "The ugly one right there."

Coral looked at the men again and back at her new sister and said, "Can you be more specific, dear?"

"The balding one who's missing two teeth," Quisling replied as she pointed at him.

"Take him to the water, sister. He's ready. Have fun and dine well," Coral instructed as she playfully slapped Quisling's ass.

"Once Captain Brady shows up, keep him entertained until I return," Quisling said.

Coral nodded curtly as she walked over to two of the sailors. She grabbed a bottle of whiskey out of the sand and poured the contents onto her body. She let the men drink from it and then said, "Oh, dear. I've spilled my drink all over myself. Clean me up with those wicked tongues."

The men obeyed as they each grasped her, licking her body slowly. Quisling used her hair to partially obscure her face. The new mermaid walked over behind Pete and wrapped her arms around his midsection and said, "Hey there, handsome. Wanna sneak off from here and go for a swim with me?"

Pete half smiled, his eyes glazed over as he replied, "Is that all that you want to do with me?"

"If you play your cards right," Quisling whispered in his ear as she caressed his member, "I'll make tonight a memorable one. You're so cute that I could just eat you alive."

Pete's mouth dried as she grabbed him by his hand and led him towards the water. He was fixated on her bare ass as she sensually sashayed her hips. She was rewarded with a groan of desire. Pete gasped slightly as they entered the sea, the cold water chilling his body, but it didn't affect Quisling.

Once they were waist-deep, the new mermaid turned around to face him. She cupped handfuls of the salt water and slowly cascaded it down her torso. Pete seemed mesmerized by her as he reached out and groped her breasts. Breathing heavily, he said, "My God, you're a beauty. I don't know if I'll be doing much swimming. I'd love to take you right now."

Quisling giggled mischievously as she leaned in and pressed her lips against his. Pete was powerless to resist the song that she hummed, and didn't notice that she was moving them both further out to sea. The hunger pangs returned full force as her body shifted into her new form, which caused her to forcefully kiss down his neck.

Quisling got in his face and coldly asked, "Do you remember me, Pete?"

Through half-lidded eyes, the sailor replied, "No. Should I? Wait, how do you know my name? Have we met before?"

"Yes, Pete. You know that my name is Quisling, but before you had Captain Brady toss me overboard my name was Mary Fairchild. The one you ratted out."

"Impossible," Pete said as he fully opened his eyes. Shock struck him like a sledgehammer to the skull as he saw her face in the pale moonlight, recognizing her instantly, but he had no will to flee, "No! You're dead! You can't be real!"

"Oh, I assure you that I'm real. And now," Quisling intoned as she shifted into her full mermaid form before his unbelieving, spellbound eyes, "I'm going to take you for a little swim and devour you!"

Pete couldn't reply as she stabbed her claws into his body and dragged him underwater. Only bubbles and blood coated the dark waters.

Captain Brady walked onto the beach with trepidation. He saw his crew were getting drunk and entangled in the arms and between the legs of the women by the bonfire. His eyes darted all around, searching for Mary. One woman walked over to him and asked with a coy smile, "Are you the one these boys call Captain Brady? If you are, remove your clothes."

"Aye, I am, miss," Brady answered, but his eyes kept hunting for the woman he'd killed as he undressed as quickly as possible. "I'm looking for someone."

"I'm someone, Captain Brady. Are you looking for me, or *her*?" Coral intoned playfully.

He looked at the skyclad woman and saw that she was pointing out to sea. Brady looked that way and saw another skyclad woman slowly meandering her way to shore. He couldn't believe his eyes and he gasped.

Mary Fairchild!

Quisling caused the captain to believe that she was a goddess of the sea. She was breathtaking as the moonlight caused the droplets of water to sparkle. Captain Brady dropped to his knees and wailed remorsefully, "It is you, Mary, isn't it? How on Earth did you survive the terrible deed that I did to you?"

Quisling stood before the shaking captain and pressed his face against her belly. She ran her fingers through his hair and murmured, "Shh, Captain. I didn't survive, but I have a second chance at a new life, thanks to you."

Tears streaked down Brady's face as he pleaded, "Just take my life, Mary. Take me out to sea and never let me come up for air. I deserve no mercy from you."

"Mary Fairchild is dead and gone. My name is Quisling and you'll remember that for the rest of your days," the mermaid remarked coldly as she dropped to her knees, still humming her song. "I would enjoy granting your wish, but that would be the easy way out. I demand penance for your crime, and you'll grant it by giving this port half of your earnings for the rest of your life."

"As you desire, Quisling," the captain uttered.

She looked at the rest of his enthralled crew and ordered, "According to my new pod, this is *our* port and we demand payment from any who harms the inhabitants of the sea or those who commit the crime that you did. You'll need to hire a new crew. These men are ours to claim. You will also feel an irresistible pull to return to this port each month and bed me here. If not, I'll find you and eat you alive. If you don't believe this," Quisling turned his head to look at the crew, "see for yourself, Captain Brady."

He saw that every single man was being eaten alive, but none could stop the women. Captain Brady could see that their faces shifted slightly, looking more like a fish with several rows of sharp teeth tearing flesh and muscle with ease. He wanted to look away, but his will was not at his command. Quisling got in his face, revealing her new visage, baring her own razor-sharp teeth and said, "Do we have an accord, Captain Jack Brady?"

Brady replied with a trembling voice, "Yes. I am yours to command and do whatever you desire."

The mermaid chuckled as she pushed the captain down on the sandy beach and sank her teeth into the crook of his neck while straddling him. Brady winced, groaning with pleasure as his member slipped inside her.

Quisling whispered, "I've marked you and now I can find you anywhere you go. You are *MINE!*"

The Ghost and the Zombie

Liz moved around the expansive cemetery, lamenting about her former life. She didn't understand why she was meant to be here on Earth, as a ghost. She didn't do anything too terrible. Granted, Liz was not a saint in life, but was this her punishment for the way that she lived?

Liz was the kind of woman who enjoyed bar-hopping with her friends after a stressful work week on the weekends. She never married, nor did she have any children. She was a free spirit in life, and now Liz was literally a spirit haunting her own graveyard.

She made her way over to her headstone and looked at the dates that were chiseled into the shiny marble stone. Liz shook her head, feeling depressed. *"Dead at 23. What a waste. If I'd known what I know now, I'd have gotten laid more often!"*

Liz could come and go as she pleased, but lately she stayed here. At first, she would wander around the nearby neighborhoods and businesses, causing mischief like moving objects around or pantsing some smug guy who thought he was way cooler than he was while hitting on younger girls.

Liz eventually got bored and would end up back at the cemetery to recharge and rest. It was exhausting to interact with the living and her surroundings. It took a great amount of energy to do things. As much fun as she had, Liz wondered what the point of being a ghost was since she couldn't do much without weakening herself for days.

She vaguely recalled how she'd died. Liz was out at a local restaurant, drinking at the bar and waiting for her food. It was early in the evening and she had already been hit on by several men looking to get her phone number and into her pants. Liz gladly handed them a drink napkin with her first name and the number (206) 569-5829.

She would giggle to herself, knowing that if the men called it, they would get connected to a radio station in Seattle and the conversations were often put on the air. Liz's stomach was growling, so she had ordered a fried shrimp basket. She greedily ate several of them at a time, but then her throat swelled shut.

Liz fell off the barstool, grasping her throat as panic set in. The bartender and several other people came over to help her up, not realizing that Liz was having an allergic reaction and not actually tipsy as they suspected until it was too late.

She never knew that she was allergic to shrimp. Liz ate plenty of seafood over the years and nothing ever happened. She looked up at the darkening sky as storm clouds threatened to empty a deluge, rumbles of thunder booming in the air.

Liz noticed a strange fog was rolling in. She found it odd that it had a blue-green tint to it and a pungent odor. The swiftly-moving fog engulfed the surrounding area as the first few drops of rain fell. People were out on sidewalks, trying to get a better understanding of what was happening with today's weather.

Uncertainty saturated the air as the rain poured down, causing people to scatter and find cover. Liz heard several people complaining that their skin was burning. She noticed that she was getting more energy from the strange weather, which was odd because normally thunderstorms didn't boost her power this much.

The ground in her cemetery got saturated, the flooding making her home look like a small lake. Liz saw movement in the muddy waters near each headstone that poked out. This confused the ghost because, as far as she knew, there weren't any animals in the graveyard. Unless it was some of the fish from the nearby pond that sat in the middle of her cemetery.

That has to be it, right?

To the ghost's surprise, a hand rose out of the water. She could see what appeared to be that person's hunched back. Liz couldn't tell if it was a man or a woman.

The person slowly stood up fully and the ghost gasped. The man was emaciated, his skin discolored with chunks of flesh missing. He only had one eye that was so pale that Liz couldn't see the iris, and the other eye was missing. The strange man slouched through the standing water like it was a normal routine for him.

Everywhere that the ghost looked more people were popping up out of the water, each looking just as physically horrid as the first man, or worse.

Liz flew around the cemetery, watching the dead rising up, until she got to her resting place. Despite her headstone being submerged, the ghost found it with ease.

Bubbles were forming in the water by it, which caused the ghost to cry out, "*No! Not me, too!*"

To Liz's horror, she watched her own emaciated form stand up on shaky, bony legs. Her wet, mud-caked hair clung to her head like seaweed and her skin was missing patches.

Liz flew around her body several times before commenting, "*Death didn't do my figure much justice. I know that I wanted to lose weight, but this is a bit extreme. Who the hell decided to dress me in all white? I look like the Corpse Bride at a wet T-shirt contest!*"

Her zombie self shuffled through the water, not paying attention to the ghost as she meandered towards the cemetery gate.

Liz looked over her shoulder at her spectral form and then back at her former body and said with dismay, "*Damn. I lost that tight ass that I worked so hard to sculpt. This isn't right. I really should have gotten cremated. I look like the undead version of a drowned Barbie raisin.*"

More zombies splashed past her, several going right through the ghost.

Liz growled, and flipped them off, "*Rude undead fuckers! I'm hovering here!*"

She noticed that her own corpse was having difficulty walking and appeared to be stuck in place. Liz flew over and ducked her head into the water. She was surprised to see that her feet were trapped in the thick mud, because whoever dressed her for her burial had put four-inch heels on her feet.

Pouting, the ghost lamented, "*Damn, those were my favorite pumps for going out. Now they're ruined! Someone could have taken them and put them to good use. Now, they're a casualty of the zombie apocalypse."*

Her zombified corpse growled as it tugged at its legs, trying to free itself. Liz got in her face, trying to encourage herself, *"Come on, Liz! You can do it! Just pull a bit more!"*

Her zombie looked back at the ghost and flailed her arms at the specter, trying to grab her.

Liz glared at her former body and said, *"No, stupid! Your legs! Work on your damn legs! Does death make a person stupid or was that reserved just for me — I mean you? Fuck, this is so confusing!"*

The ghost moved away and out of her zombie's sight. It kept trying to reach for her, but once Liz was far enough away her zombie went back to trying to free itself. The ghost watched on from behind a large gothic tombstone. She could hear people screaming everywhere and gunfire echoing off in the distance.

Liz saw her decrepit body fall forward, splashing loudly in the murky water. She giggled to herself, thinking that coordination was never a strong trait of hers in life.

Apparently, it's still a thing in death.

Liz's undead corpse struggled at first, but then it finally stood erect. It looked around several times, scanning the area as it shuffled towards the main entrance of the cemetery. The ghost followed closely behind herself as her reanimated body slouched through the muck.

The water spilled into the street and sidewalk but it didn't flood it. About an inch of the nasty water mingled with the deluge on the streets, making it easier for the zombies to chase down their victims. Liz's corpse let out a scratchy guttural moan as her bare feet touched the pavement.

Liz groaned, "*Kiss those sexy pumps goodbye.*"

Her zombified corpse locked its cloudy white eyes on an alleyway. Noises coming from there stirred Liz's former body into predator mode, her movements becoming more stealthy, but not graceful.

The ghost flew past the zombie, trying to find the one that was causing the ruckus. She had to warn them and, Liz hoped, could actually see her ethereal form. She searched all around, seeing no one. Liz was about to move on when a subtle scraping caught her attention. The ghost saw a young man cowering behind a huge green dumpster, his eyes filled with fear and dread.

Liz got in his face and shouted at him, *"Run, you dumbass! Can't you see that I'm coming to eat you?"*

No response.

Rats scurried away at the man's feet, causing him to cry out and bang his elbow on the side of the dumpster.

Liz rolled her eyes. *"Great job, dumbass! You just rang the dinner bell!"*

The ghost wanted to help the man, but if he couldn't see her then what was the point? Liz's corpse appeared in front of the terrified man, a sickly green goo dripping from her quivering mouth. Liz wrinkled her nose as the unmistakable aroma of piss and feces wafted in the alley. From the condition of the man's pants, the odor was coming from him

The ghost could only watch as her decaying old body snatched the man to his feet. She bit down on the man's neck, making Liz think of some of the vampire novels she used to love to read. The man screamed, flailing his arms at the zombie to get her off of him, but it didn't deter her. The reanimated corpse's grip was too strong for the man as his knees buckled, dropping them both to the pavement.

Liz turned around, not wanting to see what her former body was doing. It didn't help that she could hear the man's dying gasps amid the sickening gnawing of flesh and muscle. If she was capable, the ghost would have thrown up right then and there. Liz tried to flee the alley, not wanting to witness any more of this primal carnage, but after getting to the other end she abruptly stopped.

The ghost grunted, trying to move forward, but to no avail. It was like some invisible force was holding her spectral body in place. Liz had never experienced anything like this before. She glanced over her shoulder and wondered if somehow she was tethered to her undead corpse now.

How the fuck is this possible?

She decided to stay where she was and wait on her zombified corpse to finish its meal. If the zombie walked away, Liz reasoned, then it should drag her along with it. The ghost was praying that didn't happen. Her reanimated body stood up and walked further down the alley, not leaving much left of the man.

Liz could feel an irresistible pull to follow along, which made the ghost groan. She tried to resist and move away, but it was no use. Liz was indeed bound to her corpse.

"Fucking hell," the ghost growled as she glared at her zombie. *"Why this? Why now?"*

She wondered if her corpse got killed, would that free her once more? Liz was familiar with the whole zombie genre and the different tropes, but this was a new wrinkle, one that she didn't welcome. The ghost flew closer to her corpse, but stayed out of sight as the rain poured harder. Liz was curious to see if the zombie would even listen to her, or simply try to attack her like it did not that long ago.

As they got on one of the main streets in town, Liz's zombie paused and sniffed the air. It searched the area for a moment before shuffling forward. The ghost watched on as her undead corpse peered through car windows, its mouth quivering.

Liz got in the zombie's face and asked, *"Are you hungry already? Sheesh, all these people are going to go straight to our ass."*

Her reanimated body reached out, trying to grab her, but couldn't. She could see frustration on her decrepit countenance as it let out a guttural growl.

Liz put her hands on her hips and said, *"You realize that you can't eat me, right? I'm a ghost. I used to inhabit that body, ya know! Just stop trying to grab me, you're embarrassing us both."*

The zombie abruptly stopped and froze, its vacant gaze focused on the ghost, which caused Liz to pause her rant. It tilted its head, as if it was trying to remember her.

The ghost softened as she spoke, "*I suppose that if I just climbed out of my coffin then I would be ravenous, too. Are you still hungry?*"

The zombie nodded with a snarl.

Liz replied, "*Yeah, that's definitely my nom-nom response. Look, since we're stuck together, why not work with each other? I can help you find food. Hell, I'll direct you to the people.*"

"Hungry...," Liz's undead corpse uttered as it touched its withered stomach.

The ghost nodded sympathetically as she looked around. Being a spirit had a few advantages, one being that Liz could go into places undetected. She motioned for her zombie to follow her because the specter had no choice.

Might as well make the best of a gruesome situation.

Liz could see an apartment building coming into view and immediately she recognized it. One of her exes lived in a small studio that was more like a basement.

It's a fitting place for him, Liz thought as she flew near his door.

Jeff was nothing but a two-timing weasel and thought he was God's greatest gift to everyone, especially the ladies.

When Liz was dating him, she found Jeff in her own bed, having sex with two other women that she didn't know. He didn't seem to care that she was visibly upset. All Jeff said was to get in bed and join in the fun. Liz walked over to her closet and grabbed a baseball bat and threatened to break everyone's bones if they didn't leave.

The women had scattered, grabbing what clothing that they could put on while complaining to Jeff about bringing them to his crazy girlfriend's house. Jeff smirked as he got dressed, remarking that Liz wouldn't be any good in bed, let alone in a foursome.

The ghost slipped into the studio apartment and saw Jeff. His shower was running, which meant he had company. Jeff was lounging on his couch with a pair of boxers on. He was texting another woman, inviting her to come over. The emergency alerts on his phone kept chiming, which annoyed him. Several times it popped up and Jeff cleared it from his screen.

The ghost chuckled. *"I think that it's safe to say that he doesn't know about the dead rising up."*

The ghost hovered outside Jeff's door, motioning to her zombie, whistling and slapping her knees like she was calling a dog as she said, *"Over here, girl. I found a lovely treat here for you to eat. Who's a good zombie? Who's a good little zombie?"*

Liz's corpse shuffled over, slipping and sliding on the grimy, wet pavement.

The ghost groaned as she called out, *"This way. Turn to your left. No, your other left! God, my zombie self is a damn idiot!"*

Liz's corpse struggled to walk down a small set of concrete steps. The ghost rolled her transparent eyes as her decaying body tumbled down, landing hard on her face. Liz cringed as several teeth fell out of the zombie's mouth.

"*How does it feel to be coordinated,*" the ghost mocked as she shook her head. She pointed at the door and added, "*Knock on the door.*"

The zombie cocked her head to the side, trying to comprehend what Liz was asking. The ghost instructed again as she demonstrated, "*If you want the Manburger Helper on the other side, then knock on the door like this.*"

"Hungry..." the zombie rasped.

Liz reassured her former body, "*I get that. Now be a good little zombie and do as I demonstrated.*"

The zombie stood there for a moment before it reached out and knocked on the door. There was a three-second pause between each knock, which sounded like it was coming from someone that was utterly bored.

"Coming," Jeff chirped.

Liz watched as he slipped on a silk bathrobe. He checked his phone, scratching his head in confusion. The ghost figured that he must be waiting on his next sexual conquest to text him back, maybe even show up.

Jeff looked over his shoulder towards the bathroom as he opened the front door. He spoke in a hushed tone, "Sandra, you got here quick. Please—"

He froze mid-sentence when he turned his head to look at his new *guest*. The charming, perfect smile melted away as a malodorous aroma of putrefaction overwhelmed his senses. The ghost giggled when she watched him evacuate both his bladder and bowels.

The zombie firmly grabbed Jeff by his shoulders and pulled him into what would normally appear to be a lover's embrace. Liz's corpse viciously bit down on his throat, easily squelching any of Jeff's cries for help.

The ghost was sickened by the sight but she also spat, *"Looks like the player got played. I'd say rest in peace, but I hope you rot!"*

The woman in the bathroom stepped out, wearing only a towel on her head. She saw Jeff standing at the front door with someone she didn't recognize and could hear lips smacking.

The ghost observed her as she rushed over, her anger evident on her face as she yelled, "What the hell, Jeff! Am I not good enough for you that you have to make out with the next slut that comes a-knockin' on your door?"

Liz felt bad for the woman, having experienced the same scenario when she was with Jeff. The woman was about to grab Jeff by his shoulder and confront him, but Liz's corpse released him. He dropped down on the floor, twitching as blood pooled from the gaping hole in his throat.

The naked woman gasped and her eyes bulged. She turned around to run, but the zombie managed to grab her as she slipped in Jeff's bodily fluids. The two fell down on the wood floor, struggling like they were playing a macabre version of Twister.

Liz's undead corpse's fingers dug into the woman's flesh, causing her to cry out in pain

143

as she frantically hit her. The ghost shook her head as she flew outside, not wanting to witness another feeding. She wondered if her old body would ever get full.

How much can she eat? Is there a limit?

Liz could hear the woman painfully moaning for a minute before going silent. All that came from the studio apartment was the squishy noise of the zombie feeding. Rain poured harder than the ghost had ever seen, the streets looking more like swiftly-moving rivers.

The ghost watched as more zombies shuffled on by, each one in various stages of decomposition. After twenty minutes, Liz's undead corpse shuffled out of the studio. Her drenched white clothes were covered in blood and gore. The ghost followed next to her zombie, hoping that the torrential downpour would clean her off.

Gunfire rang out several blocks away. The noise caused Liz's corpse to move faster. Its single-minded purpose was to eat everyone in sight.

I guess that the entire world is now one humongous dinner buffet, Liz mused to herself as a firefight ensued.

People were running for cover as bullets whizzed past them, trying to cut down the incoming horde of zombies.

People either used vehicles for cover by standing in the flood waters or sitting inside with a window cracked just enough to fire their weapons. Liz helplessly followed along, not wanting to witness more death and mayhem. Her reanimated body rushed forward, slipping and sliding as she neared one of the vehicle barricades. Bullets pelted her body, but none of them stopped her progress.

"Have none of these buffoons ever seen zombie movies? The head! Aim for the head!," the ghost shouted, but no one could hear her.

Liz again wondered what would happen if her zombified corpse actually died. *Would I be free to move around on my own, or will I be forced to haunt where my body lies?*

She feared the latter, because the ghost didn't like the idea of being bound to one spot. It was difficult enough being forced to go with her dead body. Liz loved her independence, both in life and in death, so this had the potential of being problematic.

Liz's zombie lost her footing and fell down, the churning flood waters sweeping her down the road. Pain seared through the ghost when she was too far away from her body. Never in her afterlife had she experienced pain like this.

She equated it to someone stabbing her all over her ethereal form with tiny knives and slowly slicing her apart. Liz flew closer to her zombie as she was pulled along, which helped to lessen her pain.

The zombie rolled down a steep hill that led to the docks. People were scrambling around, trying to untie boats and make their escape out to sea. Other zombies were trudging down to the pier, grabbing anyone too slow to get away while Liz's undead corpse struggled to stand up.

The ghost wasn't sure if her zombie was injured or not, but it didn't seem to matter. Her reanimated body pushed forward, limping down to the closest dock. She had her undead gaze fixed on one man in particular. He was struggling with one of the ropes, fear making it difficult for him to concentrate as he kept looking around.

A guttural moan let the portly man know that he was being stalked. His eyes bulged when he saw Liz's zombie slowly coming for him. The man panicked as he jumped onto the boat, running for the wheelhouse. The fisherman slipped and fell, which only excited the zombie.

Liz got in front of her own undead corpse and shouted, "*Leave the poor guy alone! Haven't you eaten enough already?*"

"Hungry..." her zombified corpse hissed at the ghost as she hauled her drenched husk up onto the boat.

"*Fine! Have it your way, hippo hips!*" Liz huffed as she crossed her arms over her chest. "*Just know that this could end badly for you. Stupid zombie!*"

The ghost could hear the portly man start the engine. The boat lurched backwards rather quickly, but came to a sudden stop as another vessel collided with it. The jarring hit knocked the female zombie down, but she wasn't deterred as she stood back up.

I doubt that their boating insurance covers zombie-induced accidents, Liz mused as she saw the occupants of the smaller craft being swarmed by zombies.

The boat turned with the sound of splintering wood coming from the side. The portly fisherman put the motor on full throttle, pushing out towards the turbulent ocean waters. The ghost watched as her decaying body moved haphazardly towards the wheelhouse.

The fisherman yelled in frustration as he noticed that his vessel was struggling with the swelling waves. It didn't help that the boat was also taking on water from where the collision occurred. The portly man opened the door to go see how bad the damage was, but was greeted by the zombie.

The man turned to run, but she grabbed him by his beefy arm and bit down on it. The fisherman howled in pain as Liz's corpse pulled out a chunk of flesh and muscle. He pushed the zombie back as he scrambled to get below deck, clutching his bleeding arm.

The ghost followed the man, wondering if he was going to turn into a zombie, too, if he could manage not getting eaten. The fisherman swore as he desperately searched for anything that he could use to defend himself. He grabbed a towel and wrapped it around the wound.

Growling caught his attention as Liz's undead corpse attempted to walk down the steps, but ended up tumbling down.

"*Clumsy bitch,*" the ghost muttered as she shook her head disapprovingly.

She was surprised that her former body hadn't killed itself yet. The fisherman took advantage of the situation and managed to pull a heavy safe down on top of the zombie, pinning her to the floor.

He cursed from exertion as he sat down. "Fuck! Why couldn't it land on your fucking head? Just my fucking luck."

Water quickly poured in from any spot that wasn't sealed as the boat listed to the side. The movement dragged the zombie, along with the safe, over to the wall. She flailed her arms, trying to grab the portly man as more loose items fell from the cabinets.

"If I'm going down, you're coming with me, you fucking— Oof!" The fisherman's bitter rant was cut short as a fire extinguisher struck him on the back of his head, rendering the man unconscious. Liz watched as the cabin filled with water, submerging her zombie and the fisherman.

The boat sank into the icy ocean depths. Liz watched as it bubbled out of sight, loose debris floating in the water. The ghost had only a few seconds before the pain came on as her spectral form was tugged down into the churning waters below.

Liz tried with every ounce of strength that she had to escape, but to no avail. The salty ocean water burned just as much as being too far away from her undead corpse. Schools of fish swam past Liz, her painful wailing muffled by the ocean.

The boat came into the ghost's view. It had smashed into a large coral shelf, nearly splitting the vessel in half. Liz felt the pain from her connection to her body ebb the closer she got, but the burning never ceased. She looked at herself the best that she could and, to her horror, realized that her ethereal form was dissolving away.

As she reached the wreckage of the boat, the ghost saw that her reanimated body was still alive. Its arms were slowly flailing as it tried to dig its fingers in the floorboards to free itself. Small fish surrounded the zombie, nipping and picking off the rotting pieces of flesh. Every so often, Liz's undead corpse would snap its mouth at any fish that swam within its view.

Just as Liz's ethereal body dissolved into nothing, the ghost painfully bit out, "*I fucking told you that this was a bad idea! Stupid zombie!*"

Tales from the Fae War

(A story from *The Xander Bane Chronicles*)

"Xander Bane, are you ready to be released so that you can perform your duty for Crimson Pass?" Vestal asked.

The Dampire groaned, his body pinned to the stone floor by a circle that had been carved into it. The circle, along with the cell itself, had both demonic and vampire wardings etched into it to keep him contained. The dungeon cell had been crafted just for Xander.

The Dampire was a half-breed—part vampire and part demon, with all their strengths and none of their inherent weaknesses. Xander was three-and-a-half-feet tall and had pink skin, much like that of a pig. His slick black hair was disheveled, along with the rest of his clothes.

Vestal motioned over at another vampire and said, "Go get Hester and have her shut the magical warding off, Duglow."

"As you wish, sire," the vampire guard replied as he ran down the corridor with supernatural speed. The elder vampire looked down at the Dampire, sneering as another guard approached and said, "Is it wise to do this, sire? Why release Xander when you finally have him under control? If it was up to me—"

"It's not up to you, so don't you dare question the will of the vampire council, Ceric," Vestal coldly interrupted the guard. "Xander Bane is an abomination, but he's a tool that we must exploit."

Ceric cowered as he took several steps away, "My apologies, sire. I meant no disrespect to you or the council. It's just that it took a long time to capture him, and we lost quite a few vampires in the process."

"Your concerns are noted, but we have little choice in this matter," Vestal said as he walked into the cell, towering over Xander who was grunting in pain.

The vampiric warding caused the elder vampire some discomfort, but it didn't hinder him like it did Xander as he spoke, "The Fae are encroaching on our sovereignty. They're leaving us no choice but to fight, which puts us at a disadvantage due to the sun. Xander is the only one of us that can walk in the light. If he wants out of his cell, he *will* fight our battles during the day so we can assault the Fae at night."

The Dampire moaned, barely acknowledging Vestal. The elder vampire rolled Xander onto his back with his foot. Heavy footsteps from the corridor let the elder vampire know that the witch was here. He turned and walked out of the cell and stated, "Shut down the warding. We need him to be coherent."

"Yes, Vestal. Will you be taking him out of there?" Hester asked as she put her hand on a small panel embedded in the rock wall.

"Once the magic is off, yes," the elder vampire replied as he narrowed his eyes suspiciously at the witch. "Why do you ask?"

"I plan on reactivating it, just in case the abomination needs to be tossed back inside. It doesn't hurt to be prepared. You know that he's going to try something," the witch said.

Vestal nodded and said, "Do it."

More footfalls echoed as several more vampires came down, escorting several humans with them. The fear in their eyes revealed that they knew that they weren't going to be leaving the dungeon alive. Hester softly chanted, causing the panel to glow. The elder vampire motioned to the guards to retrieve the Dampire.

Ceric and Duglow stepped into the cell, feeling uncomfortable from the vampire wardings until it was completely shut down. They stood Xander up, supporting him under his armpits, and dragged his limp body out of the cell.

They let go of Xander and let him drop to the floor and unsheathed their swords. Hester eyed the abomination as she chanted once more, turning the warding back on. Vestal coldly said, "Get up, *abomination*. We both know that you're not *that* weak."

"Don't get your fangs all twisted," the Dampire replied as he lifted his head, smirking. "It's not like I'm going anywhere at the moment."

The guards put their swords against the Dampire's neck, hissing menacingly at him, but he wasn't fazed. He spoke to the guards, but never looked away from the elder vampire. His eyes were red, meaning that he needed to feed. "Is this really necessary? We both know that these buffoons can't kill me. That would be counterproductive, especially in the eyes of the council."

"Maybe so." Ceric forcefully pressed the blade against the Dampire's neck, drawing blood. "But you still can't be trusted, so we're not taking any chances, *abomination*!"

"This is true, but it's not like you can stop me, Ceric," Xander replied, sounding bored by the situation. "Here, allow me to demonstrate."

The Dampire teleported himself onto Hester's back, and with one fluid motion he snapped the witch's neck. Xander stood on her lifeless body, grinning from ear to ear as he crossed his little arms over his chest. Vestal shook his head in disgust. "If you're quite done showing off, the council has ordered your release with a stipulation."

The Dampire laughed. "Let me guess: it has to do with the Fae?"

"Precisely." Vestal nodded as walked up to the diminutive Dampire. "You're to go out and kill as many as you can. Since you can fight during the day, it gives us an advantage. One they won't see coming."

"And if I refuse to play my part in this trivial matter?" Xander asked, knowing the answer.

"Refusal is not an option for you, *abomination*. You will do like the rest of your vampire kin and fight. All who refuse the call to arms will be viewed as rogue deserters and will be hunted down and killed."

"I'm part demon, so technically I'm not a fully-fledged vampire. The call to arms shouldn't apply to me." Xander defiantly stuck his chin out, grinning mischievously. "As all of you here keep saying, I'm an abomination so doesn't that exclude me from the vampire community, *Father*?"

Vestal didn't rise to the Dampire's bait, so he coldly remarked, "Like I said, you have no other option. If you try to cut and run, you will be hunted down and tossed back into your cell. Since you killed the witch we can't disable the wardings, so you can rot in there, suffering for eternity or until I choose to end your life. Your life will be forfeit if you step one toe in Crimson Pass, unless we summon you from the field of battle."

The Dampire scoffed. "You and the council must be pretty desperate to ask for *my* help. What's in it for me?"

The elder vampire motioned towards the humans. "A peace offering that most of the council agreed that you deserve. Drink your fill and —"

"I'm guessing you didn't vote for this miniscule gesture of good will?" Xander stated with a knowing look.

"No, I didn't. We both know that you have loyalties to one person: Yourself. I want you to go out and kill as many as you can. I have a certain number in mind, so when I hear that you've accomplished it you may end your time in the war. If you happen to survive to the end of the war, you'll get to have your freedom."

Xander skeptically raised an eyebrow. "And this number is?"

"I'll send word when you have achieved it," Vestal said dismissively as he turned to leave the dungeon.

"That shouldn't be too difficult to achieve. I'll just imagine everyone that I slaughter is you," the Dampire remarked sarcastically.

Vestal didn't bother with a response. He motioned to the small escort and said, "Feed the abomination and see to it that he makes it to his quarters before he goes before the council."

The Dampire grunted as he rolled his eyes. One vampire roughly grabbed a young woman by the back of her neck and forced her to walk towards the diminutive Dampire. He pushed her down to her knees, causing the young woman to yelp. The vampire yanked her head to the side, exposing her neck as tears streamed down her cheeks.

"Feed, *monster!*" the vampire ordered.

Xander glared at him as leaned in against the sobbing young woman and said, "A monster I may very well be, but at least I'm not a piss-poor excuse of a vampire like all of you here."

"Just feed and keep your mouth shut, Xander," Ceric hissed.

The Dampire chuckled. "Exactly how do you expect me to feed if you want me to do that?"

"Shut it and do as you're told, *abomination!*" Ceric hissed.

"Blah, blah, blah!" the Dampire mocked as he licked the woman's neck. "Obey or else. Is that all you vampires know what to say? If so, you should really reexamine your mantra. It gets old and dull, much like you, Ceric."

All the vampires snarled and stepped forward, but the Dampire proclaimed, wagging his finger, "Ah, ah, ah, boys. No harming your weapon of massive carnage or you'll be having to explain it to the vampire council, as well as the many coven leaders all over Dragermora."

The surrounding vampires muttered and glared at Xander. The woman spoke softly as her lips trembled, "Please don't kill me."

"You're better off dying by fangs than by these cretins," the Dampire murmured by her ear. "At least I'll let you die with some dignity."

Before she could reply, the young woman gasped as he sank his fangs into her carotid artery. She groaned as she instinctively tried pushing the Dampire away, but to no avail. After several minutes, her arms dropped to her sides as the blood loss caused her to feel weak.

Ceric rolled his eyes and ordered, "Hurry up and drain her. You have plenty more waiting for their turn, and I for one don't have all night. Daylight approaches."

Xander removed his fangs from the woman's neck and said, as blood dripped from his mouth, "Don't be jealous that the council is doting on me. I can take as long as I want. They are *my* gifts to do with as I please. I know that dawn is coming soon. You get all fussy when it gets close to your bedtime. Do I need to read you a bedtime story?"

Ceric stepped up and swiftly broke the woman's neck. Xander glared at the vampire and said, "I wasn't finished with her. This is why you'll always be a dungeon guard. You have the manners of an inflamed hemorrhoid, and in this light the resemblance is uncanny."

The dungeon guard snarled as he reared back to backhand the Dampire. As quick as a blink of an eye, Xander punched Ceric in the stomach, dropping the guard to his knees. He kicked the vampire square on the chin, toppling him over. The other vampires leveled their swords at the smiling Dampire, who asked with an innocent look, "What?"

"Finish your food so we can take you back to your quarters, *abomination,*" one of the escorts said with disgust.

Xander looked at the remaining humans and said, "I'm not hungry anymore. So you lackeys can release them or whatever you wish, do your duty, and lead the way."

"Doesn't matter what you want." One vampire roughly shoved another human forward. "You *will* feed as you were ordered to do so by the council! These cows were hand-picked just for *you*. You don't get to spurn a gift from the council."

"Xander," Duglow said, frustration lacing his voice, "just do as you're told, for once. We have more pressing matters to deal with than your childish antics."

"You're so right, Duglow. Nevermind what I said. I already know how to get there myself, so try and keep up!" The Dampire grinned.

All the vampires hissed and snarled as the Dampire teleported away, his cackling echoing in the dungeon corridor. Xander reappeared on the ceiling of his quarters, looking at his meager possessions. He also didn't want to simply pop into the room without knowing if someone was in there waiting for him.

Out of habit, the Dampire did this because he didn't want to have another incident of reappearing inside a bystander.

The villagers in the middle of that town were not only surprised, but shocked by the bloody explosion. It made a gory mess, and Xander didn't want his attire soiled like that again.

Muffled voices came from outside his room, causing Xander to remain on the ceiling to see if they entered or not. The wooden door creaked loudly as a female vampire spoke to the guards posted outside, "I don't care that he's not in here yet. I wish to see Xander before his father pushes him into the middle of a war."

"Hopefully," one guard replied coldly, "the abomination falls and won't darken our halls with his presence."

The female vampire hissed as she slammed the door shut. She adjusted her blouse and jacket as she walked over to the Dampire's bed. She sat down on the edge, rubbing the silk blanket lovingly. Xander watched as she reached out and picked up one of his pillows and put it up to her nose, sniffing deeply.

The cadence of many footfalls pounded loudly out in the hall before Xander's door was violently shoved open. The vampires from the dungeon spilled into the room like water springing from a crack in a dam.

Xander shifted and hid amongst the rafters on the ceiling, easily avoiding detection with a grin.

"Where's the abomination, Vivian?" one of the vampires growled.

"I would think that *you* should know, seeing as you and your men were charged with escorting Xander Bane here."

"He managed to teleport away," another vampire answered as he opened a large armoire, pushing the impish clothes around. "He claimed that he was coming here."

"Where are *you* hiding the little imp?" the angry vampire hissed, but Vivian stood up and, in the blink of an eye, backhanded the vampire.

"Mind that tone when you address those far above your station, Corvin." Vivian bared her fangs next to his face. "If you recall, I'm a countess with a sizable army at my command. It would be unfortunate if my children weren't

165

available when the many armies of the Fae come here and storm this stronghold. I'll be sure to let the council know that *you're* the reason I don't intervene, unless..."

"Unless what, Countess?" Corvin asked, but didn't dare look her in the eyes.

Vivian slowly walked around him, causing Xander to stifle a chuckle as she ran her hand along his body. "As you can clearly see, Xander isn't here. If he turns up, I'll take my betrothed to the council when he's properly attired. I'll tell them that I persuaded him to come with me willingly, which would account for your absence."

Is she still droning on about us being together? That's just a power play by my father so he can acquire more territory, the Dampire mused to himself, his brow furrowed.

"Further," Vivian added, "I'll overlook your slight against me. Then you won't have to explain my absence to Vestal when the time comes. Do we have an accord, Corvin?"

Corvin grumbled as he replied, "Yes, Countess. Come along. Let her deal with the abomination."

The vampires left the room one by one, and then Corvin slammed the door shut. As the sounds of their boots lessened and all was quiet, Vivian smirked as she glanced up at the rafters. "You can come out now, dear. They're gone now."

Xander dropped down from the ceiling, landing on the floor without making a sound as Vivian sat down on the edge of his bed. She patted the mattress softly as the Dampire grabbed his sword from the side of the bed. "You always did have a way of controlling unruly vampires."

"All but one." The countess smiled at Xander. "Tell me, are you really going to go to war for your father?"

Xander snorted in disgust. "Like I have a choice in the matter. Either I fight or get tossed back in the dungeon. They really should just kill me, but none of them have the balls or the skills to accomplish that."

"What if you did have another option?" Vivian asked as she reached out for the Dampire as he attached his sword to his waist. He eyed her with skepticism, knowing exactly what she was about to propose.

"Do you really believe that the council would allow me to run off with you? You know that isn't going to happen. You would be just like me: an outcast. One with a bounty on that pretty little head of yours," Xander stated.

"My children would keep us safe from—"

"No," the Dampire cut her off. "It's not fair for you to risk your life and your coven for me."

"I will have a bounty on my head anyway, so why not join me, Xander?" Vivian sadly replied.

"So, you plan on rejecting the call to arms?" Xander replied with a hint of surprise. "That's your choice, Vivian, but be prepared to keep looking over your shoulder. Every vampire will be looking to take your pretty head."

The countess wrapped her arms around Xander and said with a pout, "Is there nothing I can do to persuade you to come with me? You know that you've been promised to me by your father. Surely that will prevent him from coming after us both."

"You don't know Vestal like I do, Vivian. It wouldn't stop him at all. Why marry us when he could overwhelm your territories and take it for himself? He might let the Fae wear your defenses down before striking the final blow. He would use it as an excuse to weasel his way into your court and have us both assassinated and blame it on the Fae."

The countess leaned back, holding the Dampire by his small shoulders, eyeing him intently. "I don't like the idea of you going into battle for these fools. You belong to me, Xander, and I will let him know that when we go see him!"

"It doesn't matter what you want," Xander replied in a bored tone. "The council has already decided my fate. They want to unleash their weapon of chaos because they know that I'm a monster and can do far more damage than they can, combined."

"You're not a monster. I truly wish that you wouldn't refer to yourself as such," Vivian admonished.

Xander shrugged his shoulders slightly. "If the fang fits, as they say. Come along, darling. We mustn't keep the council waiting. I'd hate to be considered rude before they have me butchered on the battlefield."

The countess stood up, masking her emotions as she strolled towards the door. When she opened it, the guards glanced at her and then sneered at the Dampire. He was grinning from ear to ear, not caring one bit about them or anyone. Vivian was expecting one of them to speak, but all the guards did was glare maliciously at Xander.

"Quite popular amongst your clan, I see," the countess remarked as they rounded the corner.

"I don't think I can say that I'm part of this clan, other than by lineage by default," the Dampire answered as more vampires hissed his way. "But I'm sure that they do love me in their own way."

"This is exactly why you should join me," Vivian muttered just loud enough for him to hear. "You would be safe at my side."

The Dampire snorted loudly, "Oh, is that a fact, my dear? I'm sure your clan will welcome an abomination into their midst with open arms."

"I'm their maker, so my laws are absolute. You *won't* be harmed or I'll have them burned at dawn!"

"It's not whether they will follow the rules," Xander countered. "I'm an abomination. Something that doesn't belong, let alone existing. No matter where I go, I'll always be seen as such. I know for a fact that several of your people feel this way."

Vivian gasped, "I had no idea. Who are they so that I can deal with them properly?"

"None that you need to worry about." Xander patted the countess on the small of her back. "Let's just say that they'll never bother me or anyone else ever again."

Vivian nodded, anger on her visage as they approached two large double doors with several guards on either side. Before the countess could speak, the Dampire called out, "Your favorite beast is here to see the council! So be good little leeches and let us into Sanguine Hall!"

The guards, unfazed by Xander's goading, opened the doors and replied coldly, "You're expected, Master Bane."

The duo walked in and approached the council. The room was cast in shadows, adorning painted images of the great vampires that once resided here and of those that still did. Artisans hand-carved the many pillars, as well as the receding rows of flat seats.

The council sat on an elevated platform made of the same stones of the mountain. It was decorated with an image of a crimson road leading into a fanged maw that dripped blood. Two Fae emissaries were standing before them, each one discussing the subject of Crimson Pass and its usage during the war.

The fae on the left had jet black hair and dark skin, almost a bluish/purple pigment, and was clad in black clothes from head to toe. In contrast, the fae on the right had long, wispy white hair and pale skin, lighter than a normal vampire, and wore colorful clothes of orange, red, and yellow all over.

Both fae ceased speaking and turned to look at Xander and the countess. The dark fae curled her lips in disgust and asked, "What exactly is this *thing*?"

"Someone that can easily wipe the floor with your boney ass," the Dampire replied with a bored expression.

"You don't have the talent or the skills to best me, imp! I'll cut you down before you can touch your sword."

"I'm sure that you have a little bit of skill with a blade, and the obvious height advantage." The Dampire smiled as he touched the dark fae on her leg, causing her to flinch back. "But I'll just chop you down like a dying tree and then take your arms off before I take your pretty little head as a trophy. The name is Xander Bane. Remember it, because you'll be screaming it when I gut you like a fish."

The light fae smirked slightly as he turned his attention back to the council and said, "Our offer is good and just. Grant my people safe passage through here and we can help keep the vermin off your doorstep. All we ask is that you don't attack us and compensation for the protection as you slumber during the day."

"I see, Fal'destion," Vestal replied with a deadpan expression. "Villenare, what is your counter-proposal from your people?"

"Give us Crimson Pass or we will simply bury you alive. Unconditional forfeiture of this stronghold is the only viable way to survive," the dark fae coldly stated with a sneer. "We will allow you and your ilk to vacate, but if anyone attacks my people the deal is as dead as you are. You *will* be slaughtered."

"Well," Xander said as he walked forward with his little arms behind his back, "both offers sound reasonable. I say go with Fal here. At least I can get some rest and not have to fight."

Villenare chuckled. "Do that and his people will kill you in your sleep. At least we are offering the better deal on the table."

The council members spoke softly amongst themselves for a few minutes. Vestal stood up and said, "Dawn is approaching, so we must go rest. Our answer will be delivered to you by Xander Bane. This meeting is at an end. Go outside with your respected clans and await our choice."

"Why not answer now? Why send that *thing*, when we both know that the council has already made up its collective mind?" Villenare demanded.

"She has a valid query," Fal'destion stated as he slightly nodded his head. "But we will *both* do as the council requests."

Both fae turned around and walked out of Sanguine Hall. As the double doors closed, Vestal glared at Xander as he asked the countess, "Why did you bring him before us? Where's his escort?"

"I gave them a break from his antics," Vivian answered as she stepped up behind the

Dampire, placing her hands on his shoulders. "Xander was misbehaving, as usual, so I suggested that I would escort him here. Since he's my betrothed, I knew that he would willingly come with me."

The muscles in the elder vampire's jaw twitched. "I never agreed to this *union*."

"You did when we made our bargain long ago. The next male vampire that you sired would be mine," Vivian said, knowing that Xander's father wouldn't like it.

"I didn't sire this one! The *abomination* doesn't count!" Vestal growled.

"Oh, but it does. You might not have sired him in the normal sense by turning him, but you did sire him through childbearing. An amazing feat, seeing as we all know that it shouldn't be possible for that to occur."

"Which is why he's an abomination," one of the other council members piped up. "Xander Bane shouldn't exist. He's a blight on our kind and should have been destroyed at birth!"

"This is true, and now it's this same abomination that's needed to protect you cowering old corpses," the Dampire smugly replied. "Please, *Father*, do enlighten all of us here as to why you couldn't kill me when you *sired* me."

The elder vampire sat back down in his chair, declining to answer the Dampire. He glanced at the other members of the council and said, "Go out there and rid us of the vermin that's trying to take our home from us all. Let your blade be our voice and make sure that they know never to come to Crimson Pass ever again."

"How many of the Fae are out there waiting for him?" Vivian asked.

"The number doesn't matter," Vestal replied dismissively. "Go out and do your duty."

"The only duty I have is to myself," Xander said with contempt. "If it was up to me, I'd gladly leave and let you all fend them off yourselves."

"What guarantee is there that Xander Bane won't do that?" a female vampire asked.

Several wispy entities appeared near the Dampire. They looked like tattered, old black cloth with many holes and tears in them. The dark entities sent ethereal tendrils into Xander's body, causing him to groan in pain.

Vestal grinned malevolently at Xander. "The wraiths will drag him back to his cell. *If he survives until the end of the war, Xander will be untethered from the wraiths and may do as he pleases. Do we have an understanding, abomination?"*

Xander gritted his teeth as the tendrils slowly pulled out of his diminutive body and said, "Yes, *Father.* "

"This is cruel even for you, Vestal," the countess said in disgust.

The elder vampire glanced at her, still grinning as he coldly remarked, "Xander can't be trusted to do what is asked of him. Think of this as a tight leash that we get to use to rein him in."

"In that case," Vivian marched up to the council, "swear a blood oath to it."

As one each council member hissed, but it didn't deter the countess as she continued to address them while slowly pacing back and forth. "Like father, like son. If he can't be trusted then neither can you, Vestal, or any of you, to do the right thing. If Xander Bane fights for the vampires in this war, and survives until it ends, he should have the freedom to do whatever he wants afterwards. I'm sure that knowing that his neck won't be on the chopping block or back in that dreadful dungeon cell would only serve as incentive, if he knows that you won't have the option afterwards."

"Out of the question," Vestal intoned vehemently. "Why should he be granted anything at all?"

"Well, for one thing," Xander walked up next to Vivian, "you *did* make that promise to me when we were in the dungeon. Don't take my word for it, ask the guards. Oh, and one other addendum. I want to rest somewhere other than here. I have a feeling that, despite my willingness to fight, I won't be welcome back here with open arms, since you made that clear. Might as well make this a binding deal or else."

One council vampire leaned forward, suspicion in his crimson eyes. "Or else what, *abomination?*"

Vivian spoke up. "I'll withdraw my forces from the playing field and let the other covens know that this council can't be trusted to have their best interests in mind. Many coven leaders will fight, but won't aid Crimson Pass. I'll see to it, because many have loyalties to me and my grand coven. Your choice."

"What's the verdict of this decrepit old group before us?" the Dampire smugly asked, knowing full well that the countess put them in a no-win situation.

"Do you expect us to grant you land and your own hovel?" Vestal sneered at the thought.

"No. It's war so I can simply take one, whether it's occupied or not. I do deserve some downtime, as needed, and I *will* take it.

I'd rather not have anyone here know of its location, though the wraiths will still be able to retrieve me. So, do we have an actual deal or not?" the Dampire asked, sounding bored by the politics.

The vampire council members looked at each other for a moment before they all stood up in unison. Vestal growled as he and the rest of the council came down from their elevated platform. They each cut their palms with a dagger that one of the council members had and then handed it to Xander.

The Dampire cut his own palm and extended his little arm so the other vampires could hold his hand. As Vestal spoke his vow, Xander glanced at the wraiths and said, "They need to do it as well. No loopholes, *Father*."

The elder vampire grumbled as he ordered, "Come forward."

Blood dripped on the stone floor as the otherworldly entities wrapped their wispy tendrils around everyone's hands. Everyone, including Xander, shuddered from the arctic chill that emanated from the wraiths.

Vestal spoke once again. "Everyone, repeat this vow with me. 'We, the vampire council, shall release Xander Bane from any punishments and allow him to be free, if he survives the Fae War. The wraiths shall remain tethered to Xander Bane until the end of the war or if he falls in battle. Any attempts to flee from the call to arms and Xander Bane *will* be put back in his cell until punishment by death is to occur. Xander Bane is allowed to live elsewhere, unless he breaks his oath'."

The Dampire spoke his own oath, his regal visage devoid of emotion. "I vow to fight in the Fae War until the end. Any who crosses my path with the intent of causing me harm, vampire or otherwise, shall meet with a gruesome end. I reserve the right to respite, as needed, but will answer the call to duty."

As they let go of their collective hands Vestal pulled out a handkerchief, wiping his hand off in disgust, and said, "Now that the binding oath is complete, go and never return unless we summon you. If you do come back here, you will—"

"Blah, blah, blah," Xander interrupted, sarcasm oozing from his lips. "I come back here, you'll kill me. I love you, too, *Father*. Dawn is here. Off to bed before you lose your much needed beauty sleep while I clear the lawn of the pointy-eared porcelain dolls."

Xander Bane cackled as he teleported away, his laughter echoing in Sanguine Hall. Vivian watched as the council slowly walked away. She said to Vestal, "Do you think he will be okay out there?"

"Frankly, I hope that he dies and we can be rid of Xander Bane forever," the elder vampire callously replied, causing the other vampires to nod in agreement. The countess' laughter caught them, including Vestal, by surprise, as she bitterly said as she turned on her heels to walk out, "I hope all of you get your wish."

"What do you mean by that remark, Vivian?" one council member asked warily.

As the countess opened the door, she looked back over her shoulder and said, "Daylight is upon us. How many of your people are old enough to resist the call of sleep? The shelter that this place offers from the sun is only good if you can be awake to defend it. I suggest that you keep a hand on your weapons while you sleep. If Xander falls, so too shall Crimson Pass."

The Dampire reappeared at the entrance of the stronghold, just shaded enough that the rays of the sun couldn't touch him. He saw that both sides of the Fae had a large complement of warriors at their disposal. The two representatives stepped forward when they noticed the Dampire's presence. Fal'destion nodded curtly and asked, "What's the council's decision, Master Bane?"

Villenare gripped the hilt of one of her swords, her voice filled with hatred as she said, "Is it submission or death?"

Xander grinned as he had his arms behind his back as he surprised both of them. The Dampire stepped out into the morning light and didn't burn. Xander unsheathed his short sword and announced, "The vampire council doesn't wish to bow before either of you. I'm out here because I have no choice in the matter. That said," he motioned for anyone to come forward, still grinning, "who wants to do the dance of death with me on this fine morning?"

The female fae bellowed, "Attack! Kill the beast! Kill the light fae! Raze the fortress! Leave no one alive!"

Fal'destion pulled his swords out. "Slay the dark fae and protect the entrance to Crimson Pass at all cost!"

"That's the plan, Fal," Xander said as the female dark fae charged at him.

Villenare unsheathed her weapons, glaring menacingly at the Dampire as she bellowed, "You'll be the first to die, Xander Bane!"

As she stabbed with one sword and slashed with the other, Xander teleported himself behind Villenare. With one fluid motion he cut off the dark fae's legs at the knees, causing her scream. The Dampire quickly removed her arms and then dragged Villenare to a sitting position. Shock cascaded over perfect visage as Xander whispered next to her pointy ear, "See? I told you my name would be the last thing you ever said."

The Dampire pierced her heart from behind, not giving the dark fae a chance to reply. He pulled his sword out of her torso and took the dark fae's head off. Xander licked Villenare's blood off his short sword as he eyed the representative of the Light Fae and said coldly, "I suppose you're next on my dance card, Fal."

Fal'destion set his feet in a defensive stance, using his swords like a shield. "My fight isn't with you, Master Bane."

"Unfortunately," the Dampire stated as he twirled his sword, his regal visage devoid of all emotion, "everyone wants me dead. I have little choice in the matter."

Xander teleported himself in front of the Light Fae warrior, slashing and thrusting with his short sword. No matter where his blade went, even with his super speed, the Dampire couldn't get past Fal'destion's defense. Xander teleported once again, but this time right behind Fal.

The Light Fae warrior rolled away, using his weapons to block Xander's onslaught. Fal'destion effortlessly got to his feet without a trace of sweat on his perfect visage. The Dampire and Fal slowly circled each other as magic and assorted energy bombs exploded in the surrounding area, causing the ground to shake.

"You're good," Xander stated with amusement, "and yet you haven't attempted an attack. Why is that?"

"I like the idea of keeping my head attached to my body," the Light Fae warrior replied, devoid of all emotion. His eyes darted behind the Dampire as the little imp stalked forward. Fal shouted, "Behind you, Master Bane!"

Xander grunted as several arrows pierced him in the back. The Dampire's lips curled in a sneer, his anger evident as another barrage of arrows struck him. Fal'destion watched on as Xander's diminutive form morphed.

The Dampire's muscles bulged throughout his little body, causing his clothing to stretch out. His pink skin took on a dark shade of crimson, and his eyes glowed black as each arrow was forced out of the Dampire's back.

"Part demon, I see. I sensed it as we fought," Fal'destion commented. "I can see why the council sent you out here to fight."

"I'm an *abomination*," Xander growled as he turned to face several Dark Fae archers, "Sit back and watch what a Dampire can do."

Xander turned on his heels, swinging his sword in front of him. None of the barrage of arrows made it past as he grinned, revealing his deadly fangs to a trio of Dark Fae. The Dampire teleported as his attackers were busy notching their arrows. Xander reappeared behind the middle one. He ran his sword through the dark fae, piercing it all the way through the torso, and cleaved the blade downward.

The other two dropped their bows and reached for their swords. Xander's black eyes glowed as he swung his sword, cutting off the hand of the warrior on the left. The dark fae cried out in pain, but was silenced as the Dampire decapitated him.

As the dead Fae warrior fell to the ground Xander deflected his attacker's blade, pushing it to the side. At that moment, the Dampire managed to punch his fist through the dark fae's chest and angrily ripped out his heart. Xander bit into it as the dying fae could only watch.

Xander took another bite out of the heart as he heard the clanking of metal on metal. He glanced over and saw Fal'destion was fending off five dark fae at once. Blood from several wounds seeped into his colorful attire.

He noted that two of his opponents were crouching down, stabbing at Fal's legs as the other three pressed their attack. One mocked as he thrusted his sword at the light fae warrior, "Fal'destion. Renowned weapons master. I'm confident that we'll break through your defenses and put your head on a spike."

Fal grunted as another blade swiped at his right leg; the pain from the wound didn't faze him as he retorted, "I'm sure that I'll be the one to survive your little *test*."

The Dampire appreciated the tactics that the Dark Fae were using, since they claimed that Fal'destion was a weapons master. He knew that the Light Fae warrior had skills just from their duel a few minutes ago. One thing that bothered the Dampire was the number of attackers. With that in mind and a mischievous smirk on his visage, Xander knew what to do.

The Dampire teleported himself onto the back of one of the crouching fae. He grabbed him and teleported both of them to the other crouching dark fae. Xander grabbed the other dark fae as the first one emptied the contents of his stomach and teleported once again.

Xander reappeared in front of a barrage of swords, using the two dark fae as a shield. The Dampire moved in between the impaled dark fae and swiftly gutted the rest of the bewildered warriors one by one. Xander turned around and eyed Fal'destion as he shrugged his little shoulders. "What can I say, other than that they had it coming?"

"Why would you save me?" The Light Fae warrior asked, bracing for another duel with the Dampire. "Are you looking to finish our fight?"

"No," Xander replied as his head turned to the magical battle. "But I do need to clean up this little skirmish and move on. Just know that if any of your clan attacks me, they *will* meet with the same messy fate as these buffoons at your feet."

"As I said before my fight isn't with you, but if any from my clan engages in combat with you and falls, I won't hold it against you. This is war, after all."

"This is true," Xander replied. He glanced at the Light Fae warrior and said, "Just so you know, the vampires are armed with iron swords and other weaponry. I'm certain that they will enlist daytime watchers to fend off further daytime attacks."

"You're certain of this?" the Light Fae warrior asked.

"It's what I would do if I couldn't step into the light," the Dampire replied coldly.

"Why tell me this?" Fal asked with a puzzled look on his otherwise emotionless visage. "Why betray your people by telling the enemy their secrets, Master Bane?"

"I'm just a *monster*. An abomination in their eyes, along with everyone else. I have no love or loyalty to them because they have none for me. I've been given no choice but to fight for them. Freedom is just a word used to spur creatures like myself to *want* to fight harder for a cause. If I'm being forced to fight," Xander twirled his short sword as a large group of Dark Fae marched in their direction, "I might as well show everyone what a Dampire can really do by owning the moniker they've given me and more..."

Fal'destion nodded as he used his foot to kick up one of the fallen fae swords at Xander and said, "Take this. Use it well. We shall guard the entrance to Crimson Pass as we offered to the council. You do what needs to be done."

The Dampire turned his full attention to the incoming horde of Dark Fae after catching the weapon and said, "Right now, I'm feeling both thirsty and hungry. I do enjoy it when my dinner comes to me willingly."

The Dampire's demonic form seemed to grow as he charged headlong into the battlefield.

As the sun finally sank below the horizon, vampires spilled out of the stronghold with their weapons drawn. Vestal and the rest of the council came out last, along with Vivian. The aroma of death and blood saturated the area, causing the vampires' lust to feed to grow stronger. Various body parts, internal organs, and gore covered the ground, causing the vampires to be taken aback.

Fal'destion walked towards the vampires with what remained of his warriors, but kept a safe distance. The Light Fae warrior announced, "As we agreed, my people kept your stronghold safe and let none of the Dark Fae invade your fortress. But this will be the last time we do this for you. Since you decided that Master Bane should kill everyone, just know that others of my kind *will* attempt to claim Crimson Pass as their own. My clan will leave it up to you to fend for yourselves."

"Where's Xander?" Vivian called out, panic in her voice. "Did he — did he fall?"

"One can only hope," one of the council members muttered.

Fal'destion pointed towards a low-lying area in the field near the base of one of the many treacherous mountainsides. The glow of a small fire could be seen as the Dampire tended to it. The vampires rushed down to see exactly what he was up to.

Gasps and hisses escaped their undead lips when they saw a massive pile of bodies and the Dampire still in his demonic form. Xander used his short sword to cut a chunk of flesh off one of the dead fae and skewered the piece with his blade. He sat down on one of the bodies, kicking his feet joyfully as he held the dead flesh over the fire to cook.

"It's about time you dead husks woke up. I was beginning to wonder if any of you would dare come out of your tomb," the Dampire said as he grinned, offering a severed arm. "Care to join me in feasting on the spoils of battle?"

"You know damn well that true vampires don't eat anything except blood," Vestal sneered in disgust. He glanced over at the

Light Fae and admonished, "Why are there survivors? The council ordered you to kill them all. Do you dare defy the council?"

The Dampire bit down on the sizzling flesh, causing several vampires to gag. He eyed his father the entire time as he stated, "Like you said, I'm not a *true* vampire, and yet you still force me to fight for your side. I chose to let them live to keep you ungrateful leeches safe. I'll kill whomever I wish in this war."

"The carnage he wrought should make you reconsider your alignment with him," Fal'destion said as he joined the vampires. "If you make Master Bane an enemy, what's to prevent him from slaughtering all of you?"

Vestal sneered, "He's nothing to us. A blight upon our kind. Xander Bane will *never* be one of us. He's an *abomination* — no, he's now the Abominable Butcher."

"See?" Xander chuckled as he spoke to the Light Fae warrior, "I told you they love me. You can tell from the new moniker my *Father* just gave me." All the humor left the Dampire as he coldly added, "When I say that I'll slaughter anyone, I mean it. Don't care if you're a vampire or Fae. What you see before you is what I will leave in my wake. That said, I'll be taking my leave from you buffoons. Find someone else to guard this place since I'm not welcome here."

"If you wish," Fal'destion sincerely offered, "you can come and reside with me and my people. If I vouch for you, no one will challenge it."

Xander looked at the Light Fae warrior and said, "A generous offer, but I'm going to have to decline, Fal. Once word gets around about me and my Father's new title for me, it will only create strife. I must go alone because that's my role in life. An outcast no one wants."

"That's not true," Vivian blurted out. She tried to make her way to the Dampire, but several council members held her back. "I *do* care about you, Xander. You can come and be at my side and—"

"No." Xander held up his hand, cutting the countess off, not caring about the crimson tears trickling down her cheeks. "If Vestal and the vampire council want me to be their daytime weapon of war, then I'll give it to them. I must butcher everyone, like I did here, who chooses to fight me because I don't want to be considered soft and weak like *true* vampires. I'll show you all what the Abominable Butcher is truly capable of doing."

Xander cackled maniacally as he teleported away, leaving all the vampires hissing in his wake.

A Gremlin's Antics

(A story from the Yonuh universe)

Day one of the plague

Onyx sat on a park bench, patiently waiting for the superstore across the street to close up for the night. People who walked by on the sidewalk on 82nd Ave would smile and nod in his direction, not realizing that he wasn't actually a man, or even human.

Onyx chuckled inwardly. *My glamour disguise is working like a charm.*

In reality, Onyx was a two-foot-tall gremlin. To pedestrians, he looked like a six-foot-tall, bald, black man. The little gremlin could make his glamour appearance look like whatever he desired. Tonight, he wanted to look more like his true form.

The gremlin had dark skin and was bald. He had on small cargo pants with a few tools in his pockets. Onyx liked making himself tall because he could fly, which made conversations easier and didn't sound like his voice was being emitted from his glamour's crotch.

The gremlin's yellow eyes glowed with anticipation. A night of mischief was just what Onyx needed, along with what he planned on taking for his own project from the oversized grocery store. He'd been watching and making mental notes about the routine of the superstore employees, trying to time his move just right. Onyx had the strange feeling that he was being watched, but from where he couldn't say.

The gremlin stretched several times, searching the surrounding area inconspicuously for the culprit. It felt familiar to him, and yet he didn't spot anything or anyone out of the ordinary.

As a small group of employees came out of the store, Onyx effortlessly took to the air. The gremlin removed his glamour to conceal his presence as he flew over the giant building and found his way to one of the back exits. A couple of hours ago, the gremlin went inside the superstore and disabled the emergency alarm on one of the back doors so that he wouldn't alert any workers who might still be inside.

Onyx hovered in front of the metal door, glancing around for any signs of movement. With a little bit of magic in tandem with his lock pick, the gremlin made easy work of the deadbolt. He carefully opened the door, the hinges squeaking loudly.

"Of all the doors on this oversized, capitalist-driven monstrosity," the gremlin muttered under his breath, "I had to pick the one door that sounds like a banshee in heat."

Onyx stealthily slipped inside the superstore and was greeted by the sounds of people working and their grumpy banter. The gremlin flew up to the rafters, surveying the situation. He could see people unloading the shipment of new merchandise out of a trailer, using a long metal manual conveyor belt. No one was paying attention as the gremlin quickly flew towards the double doors, but then he stopped.

Onyx's keen sense of smell picked up a peculiar odor. He flew low, avoiding detection while following the scent. The gremlin found himself before a door that had a sign on it that read *Employee Lounge*.

Onyx put his ear close to the door, trying to discern if there were people in the room. He doubted that there was anyone beyond the door, but the gremlin wasn't taking any chances. Most of humanity didn't acknowledge the existence of creatures like Onyx, but having been on Earth for many decades the gremlin knew that humans tended to kill what they couldn't comprehend.

Footfalls echoed in the hallway and were getting louder. Onyx opened the door and flew inside. The lounge had several rows of long tables and chairs, and several flat-screen TVs were mounted on each wall. Food containers and dirty napkins littered the tables, as well as several pizza boxes. The strange aroma seemed thick in the room, but the gremlin had to hide as the voices grew louder.

Onyx flew under one of the tables and clung the underside as the lounge door opened. He watched as several pairs of legs walked around. Someone turned a TV on and adjusted the volume as a man spoke, "See, Fred. This is what I was talking about."

"What's going on? Is that happening here, too, James?" Fred asked, sounding worried.

"The radio was talking about this strange pollen that's in the air," James replied.

The gremlin's curiosity got the better of him as he quietly peeked out from under the table. He watched the TV as a newscaster showed the particulates fluttering in the wind like green snow. James looked at Fred as he pulled out a pack of cigarettes and said, "I'm going to step out for a smoke. Care to join me?"

"Sure," Fred said as he followed the other employee out. "I want to see this stuff for myself."

As the employees stepped out of the lounge, Onyx scurried out from under the table. He walked over to a wastebasket and found the location of the strange aroma. The gremlin picked up a small red bag that had the word 'Doritos' boldly printed on the front.

Onyx flew over to one of the tables and dumped the contents of the bag onto it. He squinted at the strange orange triangles.

Tentatively, he picked one up and put it on the tip on his tongue. The gremlin's yellow eyes glowed brightly as they bulged with excitement.

Onyx greedily picked another chip up as carefully as possible with love in his eyes and asked, "Where have you been my whole life, my preciousss?"

The gremlin's eyes rolled back as he chewed on another Dorito, savoring its crunchy, salty goodness. He sucked the powdery cheese off his little fingers with delight. Onyx saw that there were no more chips left, so he took to the air and left the lounge just as the newscaster and his crew screamed and collapsed. He flew swiftly towards the double doors that led to the inside of the store, wondering if they had any more Doritos.

The gremlin was torn. He wasn't sure if getting the small motors from the reach-in refrigerators was worth it now, which was the main reason for being here. The Doritos seemed to beckon the little gremlin like an addict hunting for his next fix.

Before his unbelieving eyes, Onyx found the store was crowded with people. Humans were scrambling around, filling their shopping carts as though a great snow storm was approaching fast. Instinctively, the gremlin put his glamour up and flew around.

"Is it Black Friday already?" Onyx said to himself as he avoided the frantic humans.

He rounded the corner and went down the aisle that was marked *Snacks* in the hopes of finding more Doritos. Onyx's mouth gaped open at the sight of the barren shelves.

People were piling food and many other things off the shelves everywhere; nothing was off limits. Onyx flew up towards the ceiling to get a better vantage point on what was happening. The glass on both front entrances was busted out. More people were rushing inside, trampling anyone that fell.

The little gremlin shook his head while scratching it as he said, "Man, did the weatherman predict an inch of snow, or has Portland gotten weirder than normal?"

The store looked like a busy ant colony, but much more chaotic. Onyx heard several people screaming in pain before collapsing on the concrete floor. He observed as the bodies shook for a moment before small green shoots pierced through their clothes.

The gremlin got a bad feeling about whatever those plants were protruding from the dead bodies. The corpses appeared to be bloating, more so than what they should be during decomposition. A frantic lady ran her overly stuffed shopping carts into one of the bodies, causing it to explode.

Small particles that looked like spores from a mushroom spread all around. The spores caused anyone who touched them intense pain before they collapsed on the floor. Onyx wasn't sure what was going on but he knew that he had to find refuge from the pandemonium down below him. More people were getting infected and dying as many tried to escape out the front entrances.

Onyx flew as fast as he could, trying to outrun the deadly spores. The gremlin went to the back of the store and burst through the double doors. The double doors swung wildly, causing the unloading stockers to pause. Onyx flew down the narrow corridor, looking for anything that he could use or possibly come across another bag of Doritos.

The gremlin found a locked door that had the words *Security Room* stenciled in red on it. He knew that the surveillance room would be his best chance at observing the chaos safely. Onyx put his ear against the door and listened intently. He heard a man panicking as he spoke to someone, "People are dying all over the store and outside! What the hell is happening? Send help! The National Guard! What?! What do you mean that this is happening everywhere? Hello? Hello?! Damn it!"

Onyx didn't like the sound of this. He wanted to see it for himself so he knocked on the door and landed on the wall just above it. He snickered when he heard the man yelp with surprise. The door was yanked open as the employee blurted out, "Who the hell is—"

Onyx darted inside as the man stepped out into the corridor, looking for the one that knocked. The gremlin saw that more people were rushing to the stockroom, either fleeing the strange spores or searching for stuff to take. Onyx slammed the door closed and jammed the lock, using his gremlin magic.

The employee banged rapidly on the door as he tried to use his key to get inside. He shouted, "Hey! Whoever you are, you need to open up! You're not allowed in there!"

"Sorry, pal," the gremlin replied, "this spot is occupied. I need this room more than you do."

The man kicked the door multiple times in frustration but the gremlin ignored it. He focused on the wall of multiple screens, trying to figure out if it was possible to leave the store without getting infected. Onyx noticed that people were dying in different parts of the superstore.

What the hell is happening? There're no spore victims lying around there, unless...

The gremlin looked up at the tile ceiling above him and saw an air conditioning vent.

"Son of a Mogwai's testicles!" Onyx shouted.

He grabbed a nearby chair and ripped off the cushion and then snatched a clear trash bag out of a small waste basket. The gremlin flew up to the vent and tightly tucked the trash bag in it at the seams. He pressed the cushion against it, trying his best not to tear the clear trash bag, and used several computer cords to secure it in place just as the spores pooled on the plastic bag.

Screams bellowed just outside the security room, though they were muffled slightly. Even the security guard had stopped pounding on the door. Onyx figured that the strange spores had managed to get into the ventilation and were being distributed all over the superstore. The gremlin could only watch the monitors and wait for his chance to escape.

"I wish I had more of those Doritos," Onyx said out loud. "I have a feeling I'm going to be in here for a while."

The enormous parking lot had bodies strewn all around. The gremlin worked several knobs on a small control panel, zooming in to get a closer look.

"With all the money that this company brings in," the gremlin grumbled, "you would think that they could afford better equipment."

With a flurry, the gremlin used his magic to adjust and tweak the resolution. After several minutes, he had near HD quality streaming on the monitors.

"See there," Onyx proudly announced, "if Walmart hired me, they could've saved a lot of money, especially if they paid me in Doritos to do the upkeep on the surveillance system. Guess it's a moot point now."

Onyx could see that every single corpse had more shoots piercing through their clothes. They resembled bamboo in appearance, but were far more deadly when disturbed.

"Thank the almighty Doritos that I can fly," the gremlin remarked.

He saw dark clouds were rolling in with the gusting winds, and wondered if a heavy downpour would cause the spores to expel from their dead hosts.

Voices of panic reverberated just outside the security room from all sides. Boxes fell and shopping carts screeched as people were still snatching anything they could take. The gremlin didn't care. He was safe and out of the desperate looters' way. Onyx shook his head slowly in disbelief at the carnage that the humans left in their wake.

"Is this a local issue, or is this plague a global problem?" the gremlin solemnly wondered as more people fell to the floor dying.

Whatever the spores were, it was efficient in killing the host. Onyx saw different vehicles speeding out of the parking lot, running over the bodies and releasing more of the deadly spores, while other ones veered off and out of control.

The dark clouds above unleashed a deluge of rain that sounded like a muted waterfall as it hit the roof of the superstore. The gremlin kept his trained eyes on the corpses out in the parking lot to see if the heavy rainfall would set them off.

After several hours of nonstop rain, the only thing that the dead bodies did was swell up like a teenager's face with a horrid acne outbreak. Onyx saw people walking cautiously outside, trying to avoid the corpses.

"You'd think that they had the plague," the gremlin snickered to himself as he flew towards the jammed door.

He yanked on the door latch several times before it broke off, taking a big chunk of the door with it. Onyx let it drop on the floor as he opened the door.

He swiftly flew towards the stockroom, back to the side door that he snuck in. Onyx followed the ventilation ducts, trying to avoid the plague spores trickling out of the vents. The gremlin paused as he neared the exit, noticing more bloated bodies on the concrete floor. Each one had the same spore shoots covering their bodies.

Onyx landed on the wall just above the door and then he cursed when he saw the body of an employee leaning against it. "Son of a Mogwai's fuzzy nuts! Couldn't you find a better place to die? Worst customer service ever!"

He knew that the only way out the back door would mean disturbing the plague-infested corpse. The gremlin looked around the stockroom for a means of doing it in a safe way. His eyes focused on a shrink-wrapped pallet loaded with twenty-five pound bags of dog food. Onyx tore the plastic wrapping away and effortlessly, but awkwardly, picked up a bag. He hovered over the deadly corpse, trying to time the drop and figure out where to flee for safety.

Just as he let the dog food drop, a distraught female employee came running by. The impact of the bag caused the woman to jump as the spores expelled. Onyx flew away as fast as he could but couldn't help feeling sorry for her.

The female employee instinctively covered her mouth as the plague spores covered her body and the surrounding merchandise. The woman let out a bloodcurdling scream as she clawed at her abdomen, bending over in excruciating pain.

She dropped to her knees hard and collapsed, wailing loudly as the spore shoots pierced through her clothes. Utter silence fell over the stockroom. The gremlin waited a few more minutes, allowing the spores to settle before flying back over to the back door. Onyx hovered over her body, the woman's vacant eyes looking back at him.

Feeling guilty, the gremlin rubbed the back of his neck and said as he read her name tag, "Sorry, Sandra. I had no idea you were going to come through here."

Onyx turned around, but couldn't help looking back at her. His guilt crept into his mind, which made him grimace.

The gremlin combated it by angrily yelling at the dead employee as tears welled up in his yellow glowing eyes, "It's not my damn fault! Plague spores all around and you, Sandra, you *had* to go running through it like this was fucking quiet meadow? Why? Why did you *have* to go and get yourself killed? Why did I have to pull the trigger?"

The gremlin flew at the back door at full speed, busting it open as his rage consumed his little brain. The rain was coming down in sheets, soaking him instantly, but he didn't care. Onyx was so wrapped up in his emotions that he barely had time to notice a weighted net was tossed on him. The gremlin cursed loudly as he came crashing down on the parking lot, skidding to a halt mere centimeters from a cluster of plague bodies.

Onyx sniffed the netting and immediately recognized what had caught him as it spoke, "It's about time you came out of that place. We were wondering if you ended up dying, gremlin. See, boys? He's perfect for our job!"

The gremlin rolled over onto his back, glaring at his captors. Before him stood three smaller creatures. Each one was covered in fur and was the same height as the gremlin. Their red eyes pulsated as they looked down at Onyx with contempt.

He bared his razor-sharp teeth as he flipped his captors off and growled, "I have only two words to say to you fucking Mogwais! Gizmo shitheads!"

"Mind your manners, gremlin," the leader of the Mogwais sneered as he neared the net. "If the circumstances were different, I'd have no issue tossing you on top of those corpses beside you."

"Release me then, damn it!" Onyx bellowed as he clawed at the net. "Go find some humans to torment if you're that bored!"

"As fun as that would be, we are in need of your special skills," one of the other malevolent spirits stated.

"We will gladly pay you for your time if you come with us and cooperate," the leader said as he eyed the gremlin. "My name is—"

"Stripe?" Onyx cut him off with a snicker.

"Do we *really* need this vermin, Dax?"

"You know very well that we do, Hezz. We can't get in it unless this one opens it for us," Dax replied as he walked back and forth in front of the others.

The leader of the Mogwai gang introduced himself and the others, "My name, as you heard, is Dax. This is Hezz and Bord. Can you guess what we need from you, gremlin? If not, I can go into full details now or we can—"

"Just spit it out already, fuzzy nuts! I'm cold, wet, and sick of being monologued into an early grave!"

"I vote we toss him on the plague pile and find another gremlin," Bord responded as he pulled out a silver staff and jabbed Onyx with it. The gremlin grimaced in pain as the silver burned his dark skin.

"Enough of that, Bord!" Dax ordered.

"You know that gremlins rarely show themselves in this dreary world. We need this prick on *our* side if we want to leave here better off!" Hezz growled as he snatched the silver staff away.

"I'm so sorry about Bord's *uncivilized* behavior," Dax apologized to the gremlin with a small hand on his chest. "He's a bit irritable and wants to leave. You of all creatures can sympathize with our plight. We just need—"

"Money," Onyx grumbled as he glared at his captors, rubbing his wound. "You pricks need money to be burned so you can move on to whatever happy torture hell will take you. Fucking Chinese demons!"

"Something like that, but we prefer the term *vengeful spirits*!" Hezz replied, his red eyes glowing brightly for a moment.

"I bet that Spielberg movie hasn't helped your image any. All cute, cuddly, and creating gremlins like me when you pig out after midnight," Onyx snickered.

Dax's face soured, his lips curled up in disgust. "Now, what's your name and what sort of compensation are you needing to do this little task for us? Gold? Technology? Name your price."

The gremlin only glared at Bord, but his mind went back to the store and he said coldly, "My name is Onyx and I'll take payment in the form of Doritos."

The Mogwais looked at each other, feeling confused. Dax leaned down and asked, "What are *Doritos*? Is this some new form of currency that the Fae use these days?"

"Sounds made up to me," Bord snarled. "Onyx here is using it as a ruse to get free and fly away!"

Hezz said as he stepped in front of the seething Mogwai, blocking Onyx's view of Bord, "Don't mind Bord. Describe them to us. We want to leave, especially now that this world is dying from the plague."

"They are, without question, Mankind's greatest creation. Little triangle chips of cheesy goodness! You kids go get me as many bags of Doritos as you can and I'll assist you with your job," Onyx told them, grinning.

"You want chips as payment?" Dax asked as he shook his head in disbelief.

"Fitting," Bord spat. "Junk food for a piece of garbage!"

"Where are they located?" Hezz asked.

Onyx thought for a moment. He never knew of the existence of Doritos until today. They were a form of snack food so it stood to reason that they would be found in any store, unless people had already cleaned them out.

"There's none in that place. Trust me, I already looked. Maybe one of the little stores down the road has them? Can't miss them. They're in a red bag with the word Doritos boldly printed on it. Even a slow-minded dimwit like Bord can find them in the dark. Maybe!" The gremlin grinned as he jutted his chin out defiantly.

Bord growled as he moved towards the gremlin but Dax stopped him and ordered, "Go find Onyx his compensation so we can be done with this world."

"Fine," the irritated Mogwai stated, glaring at Onyx. "The little prick better be worth the hassle."

As the Mogwai stomped away, the gremlin called out, "Be sure to use a shopping bag and fill it up. I'd hate it if you lost a bag with those baby hands of yours!"

Bord stopped, his little hands clenched into fists. He stared menacingly at Onyx, who was still grinning as he made a shooing motion with his hand. As Bord walked away, Dax said, "Hezz, take Onyx out of the netting so we can find a nice dry spot."

Hezz nodded as stepped up to the gremlin. He pulled the net off by waving his hand over it, causing it to dissolve out of existence. Onyx stood up and stepped away from the plague corpses. He pointed towards a covered designated smoking area for employees and said, "That should do until Mr. Happy returns."

They carefully made their way to the smoking area, avoiding the dead corpses. The gremlin chose to walk as the malevolent spirits flew next to him. He was chilled to the bone from the heavy rainfall so the short walk helped take a bit of the cold away. Under the metal canopy, Onyx asked, "How much money will you fuzzballs need? There's an ATM over there that I can persuade to empty its contents."

"What we require is in a box, not far from here. It has a magical locking mechanism as well as a warding on it that keeps us from getting to it," Dax explained. "We've tried different methods of opening it, but each one failed. I know that your kind can make short work of it, though I'm not sure if the warding will prevent you from getting it or not."

"What exactly is being protected from your greedy little paws?" the gremlin asked as Bord flew towards them with a black bag in his hands. The malevolent spirit tossed the bag at Onyx as he landed next to the other Mogwais.

The gremlin looked inside as Dax answered, "A bag of rubies that belongs to us was stolen from us. We want them back."

"We tried tormenting the thief but she refuses to acknowledge us, unless we go after the box," Hezz added.

"I killed several of her lackeys, but she is steadfast at keeping the jewels. If I could destroy the box, we wouldn't be here making a deal with you, *gremlin!*" Bord spat.

"Mind your attitude, Bord," Dax admonished as he glared at the spiteful Mogwai. "I'll not have you jeopardizing this deal with Onyx when we are so close to achieving our goal. Is that sufficient payment or do you require more?"

The gremlin nodded and said with a grin, "So, where is this box located?"

"Follow me and we'll lead you to it," Dax replied as he took to the air with the other malevolent spirits. Onyx followed just behind them, keeping enough distance between himself and the Mogwais.

He didn't trust the Mogwais and wasn't sure if they would try and kill him by the end of the job. Unlike the movies, Mogwais tended to be malevolent creatures while gremlins preferred being obnoxious as they sabotaged things.

The rules from the movies didn't apply to either one, unless one considered the water. Mogwais reproduced more when the rainy season came and believed that it was a fertility sign. They also sabotaged things but purely as a means to torment others. They flew over the interstate, vehicles were mangled and sitting in various areas with the occupants bloating with plague shoots. Smoke billowed in different sections of the city as people scrambled around, looting whatever they could get their hands on.

Onyx could only shake his head solemnly, witnessing the aftermath of the strange spores.

Where did these spores come from in the first place? the gremlin mused as they approached a forested hillside.

As they weaved through the trees, a small cave came into view. The entrance was covered in damp moss, water from the storm cascading down it in several places.

Dax turned around and looked at the gremlin and said, "Onyx, I want your main concern to be opening the box and removing the rubies for us. We will distract the thief so she won't come after you."

"Hopefully," Hezz added with an impassive shrug.

"No pressure, right?" Onyx replied, and then he looked at Bord and added, "Just make sure that all of you are on the same page. I'd hate to be interrupted while cracking the lock because some of you can't keep their emotions in check."

"Just do what you were paid to do and we'll do our part," Bord spat, glaring at Onyx.

"The box is in the center chamber. You can't miss it, Onyx," Hezz said as he turned towards the cave.

"We'll go in first. When you hear the commotion, that's your signal to come in and get the rubies for us. Any questions?" Dax said.

"Why not send me in instead? I can grab the box and be out here before your little thief knows it's gone," Onyx asked as he narrowed his eyes, feeling like the Mogwais weren't telling him everything.

"The box is enchanted to stay in place," Hezz answered. "We discovered that the first time, which is why we sought you out. It didn't end well for our group."

"How many died?" the gremlin followed up, feeling a bit apprehensive.

"There were twelve of us," Dax replied solemnly as he waved at the other two Mogwais. "Now, it's just us three."

"So do it as quickly as possible," Bord hissed as he turned towards the cave. The gremlin watched the malevolent spirits fly into the cave quickly and silently. Onyx shook his head as he stroked his chin.

What exactly is this thief? She killed nine? One Mogwai is difficult to kill, but nine?

The gremlin set his bag of Doritos on the soggy ground and rolled his little shoulders several times. A clattering noise echoed from the cave and was followed by a booming roar. Onyx wasn't sure if he should go in or not, but seeing his precious chips urged him to enter.

"Time to see what kind of shit storm is waiting for me," the gremlin muttered, his voice drowned out by the battle.

He darted through the cave, hiding behind the different nooks and stalagmites. Onyx spotted the box but paused when he caught a glimpse of the fight down a narrow passageway.

"Fucking idiots!" the gremlin blurted out as he saw what the Mogwais referred to as *the thief*.

The creature was a twelve-foot-tall, green serpent, similar to a Chinese dragon, except that it had a female humanoid torso at the end of its tail. It was dripping water from the rows of black scales on either side of its massive body as it clattered them loudly, sending out a barrage of magical sonic waves at the Mogwais.

Onyx quickly flew towards the box and examined it before he would touch it. There was nothing flashy about it, just a rickety wooden box that had a latch on it, but no lock. The gremlin noted that there was a thick ring of salt around it, packed into a circular ring that had been carved into the stone ground.

"Damn Mogwais, trying to rob a Vouivre! What the hell were they thinking?" the gremlin said as he saw the creature breathing fire, lighting the cave for a moment.

Screaming echoed as the female part of the Vouivre cried out angrily, her red eyes pulsating brightly. "Foolish creatures! You dare return to my sanctuary and attempt to steal my *children* once more? For that, we will ensure that you *never* return here again!"

Onyx saw that the reptilian head had Bord in its massive snake-like maw. The Mogwai cried out as the Vouivre bit down, piercing him with one of its fangs, and slowly swallowed his charred body. The female part coiled next to the reptilian head as it held the two Mogwais in its hands, its claws digging deep into their flesh.

The Vouivre opened her mouth to speak again, but got distracted by a crunching noise. Both heads turned and looked at Onyx as he sat down on a stone slab, eating Doritos with a content grin.

"Don't mind me, I'm just here for the show," Onyx stated as he greedily stuffed more chips into his mouth. He lifted his hand up, holding a Dorito out to the Vouivre, and asked, "Chip?"

"Onyx," Hezz croaked out, "help us, please!"

"So, you are in league with these cretins?" the Vouivre spat as she slithered towards the gremlin. The reptilian head eyed him intensely but Onyx remained in his spot.

"Did you do it? The rubies, did you get them?" Dax asked as he was held before the gaping maw of the reptilian head.

"Do you think I would be sitting here if I had?" Onyx asked as he licked the cheesy powder off his fingertips. "Unlike you idiots, I don't have a death wish."

Dax gasped as he was impaled on the Vouivre's fangs. Before he was consumed, the leader of the Mogwais weakly uttered, "We…had…a deal…"

As the reptilian head chewed on Dax, the female humanoid reached out and grabbed Hezz by his throat. As he was lifted up by one of the main appendages he said coldly, "Your turn, thief. Any last words before you digest in our stomach?"

The Mogwai blearily looked at Onyx and said, "Kill her and I'll triple your pay."

The Vouivre growled as she ran her claws over Hezz's throat, slicing the flesh like it was butter. The Mogwai gargled as he was dropped into the waiting maw of the reptilian head. The Vouivre turned its full attention on the gremlin, both pairs of red eyes glowing as it slithered towards him.

Onyx took flight, cackling as he effortlessly evaded the Vouivre's strikes. He flew over the female head, pouring the crumbs from the empty Doritos bag onto her. The reptilian head roared as it unleashed a searing torrent of flames. The gremlin dove under the Vouivre and slapped it several times on its ass, causing the female head to hiss.

"When we catch you," the Vouivre snarled, "we won't let you die quickly like your friends did. We shall feast on you for days!"

"You sound like my girlfriend! She too threatens to eat me every time I turn around," Onyx replied as he landed on the reptilian head. He dug his black claws into its eyes as he added, "Wendigos, am I right? All handsy and needy, much like you two. Let's see if you can actually catch me, you Slytherin reject!"

The Vouivre roared as it thrashed around, trying to grab the gremlin. The humanoid part reached out, slashing wildly but missing with each swipe. Onyx caught the female humanoid part by surprise as he grabbed her by her black hair. He tightly wrapped it around her face several times. The Vouivre listed from side to side, both heads screaming in fury.

Onyx let out a belly laugh as he flew towards the exit while the Vouivre proclaimed, "You little shit! Get back here! We aren't finished with you yet, gremlin!"

Onyx came out and landed on top of the cave entrance, wiping the tears from his eyes. He looked down and all traces of humor left him when he saw that his shopping bag was missing. The gremlin searched all around but couldn't find it.

He landed on the branch of a nearby oak tree and grumbled, "You can't trust anyone, especially during an apocalypse. Fuck!"

A New Beginning

A prequel to *Into the Black*

Lilith stood on the observation deck looking out at the once bustling, sprawling metropolis. She slowly shook her head in disgust as she adjusted the breathing regulator on her chest. Everything was covered in red dust as the northern winds swirled all around, making it look like a ghost city.

She lifted her wrist that had her personal stats monitor on it to check how much oxygen she had remaining. The harsh and inhospitable conditions of the planet tended to interfere with the life-saving machinery, so one had to be constantly monitoring the gauges. If not, the inhabitants of Mars would black-out from the lack of oxygen and end up dying.

The breathing regulators were automatically recharged and refilled within the different facilities by linking with the AI technology, using the recycled air system. The citizens of Mars didn't always live like this. The planet was once teeming with life and an overabundance of flora and fauna and blue skies as far as the eye could see.

Now, it was a desolate landscape devoid of life. All the major cities and settlements were no longer standing, except for Salvation. This city was constructed twenty years ago because of the drastic changes to the environment which occurred when a great portion of the population was craving plants to consume.

It was so bad that none could decide if it was a sickness, a fanatical way of life, or both. Veganism, in the beginning, was viewed as a way to purify the body and never to consume animals because they were living creatures.

When the fruits and vegetables weren't satisfying their cravings, the Vegans ate all forms of plant life, such as the grass and all the flora. Some theorized that the Vegans had ingested a fungal parasite that seemed to override their brains, forcing them to consume more.

The Vegans were like a plague of locusts, their hunger unmatched, which led to the destabilization of the planet's ecosystem.

Nothing could grow in the soil now, and all the rivers and lakes dried up. They had eaten so much flora that their skin had turned different shades of green. The Vegans were both starving to death and slowly suffocating from the lack of properly operating breathing regulators. Depending on how much a Vegan consumed, they were able to live longer than some of their cohorts.

The harsh storms of the planet intensified, laying many cities and settlements asunder. Salvation was slowly being eroded away; the walls around it blocked not only the brunt of the apocalyptic dust and wind storms, but kept the Vegans at bay.

Lilith looked up at the hazy night sky in the direction of their one hope for redemption and a new beginning. A distant planet shined brightly and had everything that the people of Mars squandered away. The research and the data gathered from the scientists showed that it could sustain the survivors of Salvation because the planet, which they called Earth, was covered in an abundance of water and the air was pure.

One of the greatest dangers on Earth were the inhabitants. Huge reptilian creatures roamed the landscape, a mixture of carnivore and herbivore behemoths on the vast land mass. The Martians had no choice. Either stay on Mars and die or take their chances with the beasts and try to live in harmony with them, which may lead to their extinction.

The beeping on her personal stats monitor told Lilith that she had to go back inside. She turned around and briskly walked over to the door and pressed the button on its frame. The door hissed as it slid open for her as she rubbed her chest.

The environment is getting worse. The regulator can't keep up with my breathing needs, Lilith thought as she entered the facility.

She staggered slightly as she leaned against the wall, trying to catch her breath. As the AI technology synced with her regulator, the door beeped and slid open.

An elderly man stepped inside, though he wasn't as frail as one would make him out to be. He was six-foot-three and had thick wavy silver hair and a body that should belong to a muscular teenager. The man walked over to Lilith as she pushed away from the wall, her breathing normalizing.

"Taking one last look at our home, I see?" the elderly man said.

Lilith rolled her shoulders and brushed her curly red hair from her face. "Do you think I'm being foolish for lamenting already, Ares?"

"Not at all, my dear," Ares replied with a warm smile as he placed a hand on her shoulder. "It's to be expected. This has been your only home for nearly five hundred years. Don't you dare think that I would mock you for it."

"Are you still planning on staying behind? There's plenty of room onboard the ship, sir."

Ares let his hand move down to her regulator. "These aren't lasting as long as we hoped, are they?"

"Yes, but you know that," Lilith answered with a knowing look. "You're avoiding my question."

"I have no choice in regards to the mass exodus. I'm tied to this planet and still have much work to do," Ares said as he let his hand drop. He walked over and sat down on a couch and added, "Someone has to end the Vegans' suffering, and I'm the only one who can do it. I wouldn't ask any of you to stay behind, not when a new beginning is waiting on the horizon."

"It's not right," Lilith angrily spat as she paced in front of the elderly man. "If it's mercy you want to give them, why not have a small group go out beyond the walls and do it?"

Ares pointed at her regulator and said calmly, "Those will malfunction before they get to the first tribe. Not even the nanobots inside their bodies could keep pace with the horrid demands of our environment. No, it *has* to be me. I don't like this anymore than you do, but we both know that I'm the only one who can walk on the planet's surface and not be affected."

Muffled shouting and arguing just outside the room caught their attention. The door beeped and slid open as several men barged inside. A portly man, his face red, stormed up to Lilith as she stood up. He poked her in the chest and demanded, "Why am I being left behind? This is an outrage! Do you know who I am and what I've done for our people?"

Lilith glanced over at Ares, who remained seated and nodded slightly, before she crossed her arms over her chest and said, "I know *exactly* who you are, which is why you're being left behind, Senator David."

"And what exactly are you suggesting I did that would warrant me being left behind to die?" David indignantly asked, his eyes narrowed on the redhead.

"Hmm, let me think. Oh yeah, '*All is well. There's no need to panic. The environment is thriving.*' Do you recall saying those words during your many heated arguments as you allowed the Vegans to ravage our world? You turned a blind eye to their destruction all the while passing legislation to ensure that your pockets remained full."

"Now see here, woman —"

"No, you see here, David!" Lilith snapped, cutting the senator off. "Don't you dare get flippant with me. Your power to sway others only worked on the senate floor! I've got a question for you. What skills do you have that will be useful in a survival scenario?"

David stammered as he replied, "I-I-I'm great at organizing people and motivating them to work and get the job done."

"Good to know," Ares said as he set his hands on his lap. "But what about physical skills? Can you hunt? Can you grow and harvest vegetables from a garden?"

The senator looked between the two, sweat glistening on his brow as he tugged on his collar. "No. I've never had the opportunity to do those things."

"Then you, like all the other politicians, fall into the non-essential category. The inept handling of the environmental crisis, as well as the Vegans, tore down our great civilization," Lilith said as she walked over to a refrigeration unit embedded in the wall. She opened the door and pulled out a syringe that contained a green substance.

David's eyes widened with fear as the redhead approached. "Don't you dare think that I'm going to allow you to inject me with that stuff. I'll fight—hey! Release me! You work for me, damn it!"

The men grabbed the senator roughly, holding him in place. One man yanked David's head and pulled it to the side, exposing his neck. He winced in pain when the needle pierced his skin as Lilith said coldly, "It's funny how loyalties can shift when survival is at stake. I wanted to be the one to inject you with the flora toxin myself. Because of your antics, my family perished at the hands of the Vegans and to starvation. You're nothing more than deadweight, a burden on resources, and a waste of precious oxygen. Guards, take him to the gate, along with the rest of the politicians, and throw them out."

The senator dropped to his knees, gagging as he undid his tie. Lilith kicked a waste basket under his head just as green vomit spewed forth. Ares stood up and motioned for the men to stand David up.

He walked over and said to the senator, "By the time you're outside of the walls, the toxin will have taken full effect. The Vegans will believe that you're a plant and will be compelled to consume you. No hard feelings, David."

"You just signed my death warrant. I hope you all collide with an asteroid and die slowly from a breach in the hull!" the senator growled as he was dragged away, the heels of his polished shoes scuffing the floor.

Lilith wanted to punch the senator in the face but she managed to keep her anger in check. Ares got in her view and said, "You did the right thing, Lilith."

"Did I?" the redhead bitterly replied. "I may have sent him to his death with that injection, but I wanted to do more. Make him suffer longer."

"Understandable, but it's not your place. His sentence is being carried out as we speak.

Are you ready to disembark, my dear?" Ares asked.

Lilith shrugged her shoulders. "There's nothing for me here now, except you."

The elderly man smiled as he said, "Maybe so, but at least Lucifer will be on *The Ark*. I know that you fancy that little devil."

"I'm grateful for that. It will make dealing with this situation much easier. I just wish you could be with us when we set foot on Earth for the first time. Are you sure I can't convince you to come?"

"Mars is where I must remain. You need to carry on with the burden of starting over without our technology to fall back on. Which reminds me," Ares reached into his coat pocket and pulled out a silver cylinder. "Do you know what's in this?"

"Your new batch of nanobots," Lilith answered as she tentatively reached for it.

"Yes. Keep it safe from the others. This was a quick batch, so they haven't had the necessary time to properly develop," Ares said as he put the silver cylinder in her hand. "I don't know what you'll face or have to endure, but know that this will, one day, be a lifeline, when the time comes."

Lilith walked over and picked up her duffel bag and slipped the cylinder inside as she said, "The fate of future generations is depending on it. No pressure."

She slung the strap over her left shoulder as she walked towards the door. Ares slipped his arm into the crook of Lilith's other arm and escorted her out. As they quietly strolled down the corridor, the elderly man asked, "It's going to be a long journey; will you be able to play nice with *him*?"

The redhead tensed up. "Him who, sir?"

"You know damn well who. It's no secret to anyone that Adam will be in the cockpit, flying the vessel." Ares looked at her sideways and added, "Or that you two have a turbulent history together."

Lilith groaned but kept her composure. "Why bring our relationship up now? It's not like I did anything wrong. He's a thick-headed buffoon who strayed away from me."

"I just want to make sure that everyone makes it to Earth in one piece, especially since Eve is going, too," Ares said. He kept watching her, trying to gauge how she would react, as they entered the elevator.

"Would it be a total loss if Eve managed to get herself jettisoned out of an airlock?" Lilith asked with a wry grin.

"Do behave, child. I've lost so many of you that it hurts me both mentally and spiritually," Ares admonished as the elevator swiftly moved downward.

Lilith hung her head and said, "Sorry, Father. I'm not sure if I'm the right person to do this. If it were up to me, both Adam and Eve would be joining Senator David outside. I'm no leader."

Ares untangled his arm from hers and then he touched her back. "I can sympathize with your plight. Not many people want the burden of leadership. You, along with your fellow survivors, have a destiny before you. Whether it's a great one or a destructive one solely depends on the choices all of you make. I have faith that you will do the right thing."

"If you say so," Lilith replied as she shook her head.

Ares reached into his pocket and pulled out a small bag that had a capsule in it. He looked it over, carefully scrutinizing to see whether it had ruptured or not. The elderly man handed it to Lilith and said, "Take this, but don't swallow it. Just let it dissolve under your tongue."

The redhead looked at the pill and asked as she opened the bag and let it drop onto her palm, "What is it?"

"It's my last batch of nanobots. These were made before the ones in the cylinder. I wish I had more, but this was all I could save from my lab after several Vegans ransacked it."

She eyed it closely and asked, "Why not add it to the cylinder?"

Lilith put the pill in her mouth as Ares explained, "As I said, they aren't mature enough for anything at the moment. If I did it now, it would ruin them both."

Lilith felt the pill breaking down under her tongue. She closed her eyes and grimaced as the nanobots burrowed into skin.

"Are you all right? It's not causing too much pain?" the elderly man asked.

"Yes to both, but I understand why I must do this. Sort of."

"You're a vessel for this generation of nanobots. When the time is right, just add them to the ones in the cylinder. Just a few drops of blood will do."

"I see. Stop giving me that look. I'm fine, but after doing that I'm pretty sure nothing could be worse than that," Lilith replied as she used her tongue to rub the tender spot in her mouth.

She knew that her nanobots would take care of the wounds, but it didn't stop her from massaging it. The elevator stopped abruptly and the door slid open. The starship, which was referred to as *The Ark*, was built to resemble a large asteroid, with many different types of crystals and stones on the outside that could harness and store the energy from the sun to power it.

The outer shell was organically grown over the ship, using nanotechnology to ensure that it would adhere to the starship. The interior was a bare bones cargo ship, with individual compartments to put the bulk of the survivors in suspended animation.

The Ark had several fusion reactors that took the energy gathered in the crystals from the outer hull along with a direct fusion drive to aid with propulsion and give the ship more than adequate thrust to escape Mars' gravitational pull and get to Earth in a timely manner.

People were being herded up a long cargo ramp, each person carrying one bag of both personal and essential items for the long mass exodus. Standing just outside the elevator were Adam and Eve.

Lilith rolled her eyes and flatly commented, "I stand corrected. Adam."

"Lilith." Adam nodded curtly.

"Hello, Lilith," Eve said warmly.

"Hello, *shiksa*," Lilith replied indifferently as she tried walking past them.

Ares groaned, shaking his head as he stepped out of the elevator, knowing that this would end in a fight.

Adam roughly grabbed Lilith by her upper arm and demanded, "What's your damn problem, woman! That was rude of you to call Eve that name. I want you to turn around and apologize right now, or so help me I'll — "

"You'll do what exactly?" Lilith yanked her arm free as she defiantly jutted her chin out. "Beat me? Brow beat me into a submissive, obedient lady who will tend to your every whim? You can try but I guarantee that you won't be walking on the ship, but crawling aboard."

"It's okay, Adam." Eve touched his shoulder, trying to keep the peace. "I'm okay — "

"You might be, but I'm not," Adam gruffly interrupted her, forcefully pulling away from Eve's touch. "Apologize now!"

Lilith replied with little emotion, "Watch it, Adam. Your balls don't match that macho bravado of yours. Never has and never will. I'll never apologize, and there's nothing you can do about it."

Adam roared as he threw a right hook, aiming for the redhead's jaw. Quicker than a heartbeat, Lilith caught his arm as she sidestepped and painfully twisted it. She was surprised as much as everyone there, except for Ares who smirked slightly. Eve cried out, begging for Lilith to let go of Adam as he dropped to his knees painfully groaning.

"Don't hurt him," Ares said as he stepped up next to Lilith. "You need him to help fly the ship."

"You know better than to raise a hand to me. This is exactly why I left you. I'm not a meek, weak-minded fool you can toss around. I fight back, and right now I feel like I can rip your arm off and club you to death with it."

Alarms rang out from high above and froze everyone in their tracks. A young man came running towards Ares with a panicked expression on his face and shouted, "They've breached the walls! The Vegans are swarming within the cloister!"

"Are you sure of this, Burke?" Ares asked, feeling confused and astounded.

"Yes, I'm sure!" Burke shrieked with wide eyes. "I barely got away! The people they caught, well, they overwhelmed them and ripped out their lungs. They ate the lungs! The fucking lungs because they can't breathe!"

"Burke," Lilith ordered, "get to the ship now. We're leaving in about a half-hour."

An explosion nearby rocked the hangar, causing debris to cascade down everywhere.

Ares stoically said, "More like ten minutes, if you're lucky. Release Adam so he can get *The Ark* ready for takeoff. Eve, make sure everyone is safely secured onboard. You too, Burke."

"We'll never make it!" Burke shouted as he fled the hangar as more screams could be heard. As Lilith let go of Adam, he and Eve sprinted to the starship.

Ares looked at the redhead and said, "Do you want to see what other changes the new nanobots did to your system?"

She looked at the elderly man and warily asked, "Why do I get the feeling you didn't want the others to see?"

"You're correct, because I believe that you'll cause more terror than the Vegans. Your body is now a weapon. You demonstrated superior strength and a certain level of apathy that a predator has for its prey."

"What are you saying, Father?" Lilith asked as pounding on several doors echoed loudly.

Ares pointed at one and said, "The new nanobots inside your body are programmed for the self-preservation of the host. If you are threatened, your body will change to meet the threat head-on. I'm not entirely sure what will occur, but they won't stand a chance. Keep them busy until it's time to take off."

"Okay, but what will keep Adam from simply leaving me behind?" Lilith shouted.

"I'll speak with him and let Adam know. Trust me, he won't disobey me on this matter. Now, go!"

Lilith nodded and turned towards the nearest door. She ran over to it and discovered that, despite being at least a thousand feet away, she somehow got to the door in two seconds. The door bucked violently as the screws holding the hinges broke and gave way. As the door opened, Lilith cried out angrily as she ran at the first wave of Vegans, swiping her bare hands at anything that moved.

Thick green blood sprayed everywhere as the redhead cut the Vegans down with her three-inch claws. Lilith was consumed with rage and the singular purpose of keeping everyone safe aboard the starship. She looked down at the exposed neck of one of Vegans, and instantly her teeth elongated into a pair of fangs.

Instinctively she viciously bit down on the man's neck, causing him groan in pain. Several of the Vegans grabbed Lilith, trying to get her on the ground, as one was demanding,

"Give us your lungs, bitch! We can't breathe without them!"

She felt her body being stabbed repeatedly, but she didn't flinch or let out a sound from it. Once she drank her fill of the Vegan man, Lilith let him crumple on the floor. She spun around faster than Martianly possible, her arms freeing her from her assailants' grip and breaking their arms at the same time.

Lilith eyed them all and coldly stated, "You don't need my lungs to breathe because you're already dead, you just don't know it yet. But I'll remedy that."

She charged headlong at the Vegans, killing indiscriminately, as Adam's voice called out to her over the intercom, "Lilith! The ship's ready to launch. Get your ass on board, now!"

The redhead knocked four of the remaining Vegans out and tossed them into a freight box. She lifted it effortlessly, which surprised Lilith as she sprinted towards *The Ark* without breaking a sweat. More Vegans came tumbling into the hangar as another set of doors gave way to their onslaught.

As she marched up the cargo ramp, Ares saw her and gasped, "Lilith? My child, are you okay?"

"Never better, Father," she answered as she dropped the freight box down without a care. She looked at him and said, "I'm not sure what your new nanobots did to me, but I love it. Have you changed your mind? Are you coming with us?"

As the ramp rose, several female Vegans clambered onto it, trying desperately to get inside. Ares backed away and said, "My place is here on Mars, my child. You take care and guard the cylinder with your life. They aren't ready for them yet."

Lilith nodded curtly as the elderly man disappeared before her eyes. She was the only one to ever witness this ability of his. The man, if you could call Ares that, was tied to the planet and wasn't strong enough to leave it, especially after what happened to the environment. It hurt the redhead that Ares would be left behind and all alone, but she understood why.

As the loading ramp closed, two female Vegans slid off and onto the metal-grated floor while several more got cut in half. The two females stood up as the starship launched into the air, maliciously eyeing the redhead. Lilith smirked as they both pulled out a knife and charged at her.

She didn't bother defending herself. Lilith watched on as the blades kept sliding into her body. A slight pressure was all that she felt as she grabbed one of the females by her dirty hair and snapped her neck.

"Why won't you die?" the other Vegan hissed as she slashed at Lilith's neck, hoping to get lucky and hit her carotid artery.

The redhead snatched the Vegan by her arm, easily breaking it like a twig. As she cried out in pain, Lilith held the woman against her body just as the door to the cockpit opened. The inertial field powered up and covered the outer hull as Eve stepped out to see what all the commotion was about. The sight froze her in her tracks.

To her horror, she saw Lilith biting down on the Vegan's neck. The redhead's eyes glowed red as she stared at Eve like she would have her next. The female desperately punched Lilith in her face, trying to get her off, but the blows didn't faze her.

Eve stifled a gasp and covered her mouth in horror, watching the Vegan female go limp. Lilith released the woman, letting her corpse drop at her feet. A loud explosion from somewhere outside the starship caught their attention. The redhead walked over and looked out one of the portholes and saw Salvation, the last city on Mars, crumbling to its foundations.

As the dust settled before *The Ark* broke through the atmosphere, Lilith thought that the ruins of Salvation resembled a giant face staring back at the starship as it left the planet.

"Goodbye, Father," Lilith whispered as she placed the tips of her bloody fingers on the window.

A single tear trickled down her face as another gasp caught her attention. Adam wore a look of shock and revulsion as his eyes looked Lilith up and down.

Her body was saturated with the thick green blood from all the Vegans she'd killed. Her form-fitting jumpsuit was covered in punctures from the various knives used against her, yet no wounds were visible. Lilith's eyes were wildly glowing as she maniacally smiled at the couple, her fangs more pronounced and with more of the Vegan blood dripping off them.

"What in the name of the Creator is the matter with you?" Adam demanded, but his bravado wavered when the redhead chuckled coldly.

Eve meekly poked her head from behind Adam, using him as a shield, and asked, "Lilith, have you gone mad?"

"There's nothing wrong with me," Lilith replied as she ran her fingers over her clothing. She slowly sucked the Vegan blood off as she added, "I've never felt more alive than I do now. I feel the need to feed, but not on the food in storage."

"What do you hunger for?" Eve gulped as she slowly backed into the cockpit.

Lilith tapped the freight box with her foot, causing the occupants to bang and scratch at the lid. "I have a couple of meals in here."

"And if you finish those Vegans off, what will you feed on?" Adam asked warily.

Lilith ran her tongue over her lips and her fangs. "Let's just say that it would be prudent to increase the speed of the ship, because if I need to feed both of you *will* be next."

Eve let out a shrill scream as she took control of the navigation system. Adam slammed the door and locked it just as the redhead rushed at him. She punched and pounded on the door, putting dents in it that could be seen on the other side.

Eve frantically put the fusion drive into full throttle, violently lurching the starship forward. Adam had little time to react as he was thrown back against the dented door, despite having the inertial field running.

Beyond it, the muffled voice of Lilith was spewing obscenities as she was tossed back further in the ship. Eve's hands were shaking as she tried desperately to slow *The Ark* back down to a reasonable speed.

"Adam!" Eve shouted. "I need your help here!"

He grunted as he held the back of his head. Dazed, Adam asked, "What's happening? Where did Lilith go?"

"Who cares! She's—" Eve replied, but got interrupted by a loud siren blaring overhead. She looked at Adam and asked, "What's that noise?"

Lilith groaned as she stood back up, the overhead alert system's high pitch squealing making her ears ring. She walked over to a control panel and turned on the view screen to see what was causing the alarm to go off. Her eyes widened and she gasped. Lilith turned around and ran back towards the cockpit.

"Proximity alert, I think, but that can't be right." Adam stood up on wobbly legs. He attempted to get to his seat but he collapsed.

"Nothing is that close to our trajectory. Eve, what do you see? Is it an asteroid?"

"No, we're coming up on Earth," Eve said with a quivering lip.

"Impossible," Adam said as he crawled on the floor. "It's too soon to—"

"Damn it, you two!" Lilith snarled as she smacked the door. "You two buffoons have us on a collision course with Earth! Slow the ship down or change course, now!"

Adam clawed up and managed to roll his body onto the chair and strapped himself in. Looking at the gauges and seeing the planet growing larger by the second, he anxiously pressed buttons. He attempted to pull the throttle back to slow the starship down, but there was too much resistance. Adam barked at Eve, "We're coming in too fast. Fire the emergency buffer bubble, you ignorant girl!"

Eve frantically looked around for it, which irritated Adam as he shouted, "The yellow flashing button in front of your useless face. Hit now, woman, or we will all be dead!"

Eve flinched but managed to hit the right button, releasing a large translucent ball of energy that sped towards the surface of the Earth. Adam wasn't sure if the buffer bubble would be fully stabilized and solidified enough to halt *The Ark* from impacting the planet at this deadly speed.

Lilith ran back over to the control panel and buckled herself into the chair as she watched the viewer screen, seeing everything from the cockpit's perspective. The outer layer of the inertial field glowed bright orange as the starship entered the Earth's atmosphere.

Lilith nervously watched as the emergency buffer bubble deployed from the nose of the ship. It flew ahead of *The Ark* towards the rapidly approaching land mass. The redhead chewed the inside of her cheek, wondering if anyone, including herself, would survive if the buffer bubble didn't fully solidify.

She got the sensation that she would live, but it would require a lot more blood. She nodded, knowing that the new nanobots were somehow communicating with her. She clenched the arms of her chair and tensed up when she saw the buffer bubble coming into view and knew that it wasn't fully ready to absorb the impact.

The starship hit the buffer bubble with enough force that it managed to pierce it, causing a fiery explosion around the epicenter. Plumes of dust, smoke, and debris kicked up in the air, blocking out the sun. Fires burned all around the impact crater near *The Ark*.

Sparks from different electrical components popped all around Lilith as she scrolled through the cameras that still operated. She gasped when she saw many of the enormous reptiles staggering and listing before falling to the ground.

Each one was dying an agonizing death from not only the debris kicked up from the impact, but the dramatic drop in the Earth's temperature. The readings on the screen showed the heat signatures of the mighty beasts. One by one, the red dots on the screen disappeared. The redhead furiously typed on the console, getting more readings about the planet and to verify that the reptilian inhabitants were dead. According to the data coming through the scans, the crash had inadvertently created an extinction level event.

Lilith ripped the safety straps off, not bothering to unfasten them as the door to the cockpit groaned halfway open. Adam stepped out, holding his head, with Eve crying as she meekly followed behind him.

Slow clapping caught their attention as Lilith glared at the duo and said, "Way to go. You two have managed to single-handedly kill off the reptilian inhabitants of this world and wreck the ship. Tell me again why you two were picked to fly us to Earth?"

Adam grabbed Eve roughly as he retorted, "Blame *her*! She's the one responsible for the mess that we're in, but I suppose that I should add you to it, too."

"Me?" Lilith raised an eyebrow suspiciously. "How is this crash my fault, when you two were locked in there?"

"It's not her fault—" Eve said, but the painful vise grip Adam had on her arm silenced her.

He sneered at the redhead. "Your hideous transformation scared Eve, which led her to put the fusion drives at maximum speed. If she's to blame, then so are you, *demon*!"

In less than a beat of a heart, Lilith rushed at Adam and punched him in the gut. He dropped to his knees, gasping for air. Eve attempted to plead with her, but Lilith backhanded her along her jaw. She crumpled to the floor as the other survivors slowly shambled out of their stasis pods.

Lilith leaned down and roughly grabbed them both by their hair and intoned, "Save the blame games for your *shiksa* here and anyone else who actually gives a damn about what you have to say. I never once believed that I was wrong to end our short-lived relationship, Adam. You might want to repair what you can of this ship. You and the survivors will need it as a shelter until the calamity you two brought down on this world dissipates."

Lilith walked over to the control panel and engaged a biosphere shell that would not only encase *The Ark* and nearly fifty-eight thousand square miles, but also create a safe environment for the rest of her people. She lowered the loading ramp and grabbed her bag that contained the cylinder of nanobots.

As the redhead moved to leave, Adam got up and roughly grabbed her by the arm and demanded as he clutched his stomach, "Where do you think you're going? Everyone is going to be needed here if we are to survive this!"

Lilith effortlessly yanked her arm away from his grip. She grabbed Adam and roughly pinned him to the wall, her deadly fangs dripping with saliva. "You still don't get it, do you? You have no sway over me. If I wanted to, I could easily rip your fucking throat out and bathe in your blood."

All of the anger in Adam's face switched to sheer terror as she ran her claws across his chest. Lilith reared back to stab Adam, but a firm hand touched her shoulder. The redhead quickly turned her head, glaring at the one who was holding her back.

"Lucifer," Adam pleaded, "talk some sense into her, please!"

"Why should I?" Lucifer replied with an amused smile. "This could be quite therapeutic for Lilith. I'm more curious to know if she guts you like a fish, will she use your intestines as a trophy or a jump rope? What did you do *this* time to warrant her ire?"

Eve gasped. "You're not going to stop her?"

"Adam needs to learn that there are always consequences to one's actions," Lucifer replied as he ran a hand through his long, silky blond hair. He looked into Lilith's red eyes and asked, "What did this buffoon do?"

"He and his little trollop crashed the ship, killed an entire race in the process, and then had the nerve to blame me for it and are now demanding that I stay here and clean up *their* mess!" Lilith snarled as her emotions ran rampant.

Lucifer tsked as he beckoned the redhead to come to him. She looked at the other survivors as they entered the area. They all had a similar look of terror and disgust on their faces. Lilith knew that it was because of her new transformation from the nanobots.

She released Adam, letting him collapse to the floor. Eve rushed over to soothe him as Lilith leaned against Lucifer.

He guided her towards the loading ramp and said, "Come along, my dear. This isn't a place for either of us. Let them fend for themselves."

Lilith leaned down and grabbed the handle of the crate and dragged it with them as more pounding came from inside it. She looked warily at Lucifer and asked, "Why aren't you afraid of me? I'm not the same woman that you remember back on Mars."

"Ares told me about the little upgrade with the new nanobots before we left Mars. Though you do appear different, I'm still okay with what I see before me, Lilith," Lucifer replied honestly.

Adam bitterly yelled out, "You two deserve each other! You're both *monsters* and shall never be welcome here! Devils, the both of you!"

"Sometimes a monster is needed instead of a witless man," Lucifer retorted. "Unlike you, I know how to cherish those around me."

"Enjoy your little garden of Eden here," Lilith spat, glaring as they stepped down the ramp. "If any of you come looking for us, I'll drink you dry!"

The duo walked off the starship, arms interlocked, as the remaining survivors huddled around both Adam and Eve, wanting to know what had occurred and how to handle their new environment and situation.

The Invitation

Amy Shiller swung her sledgehammer at the remnants of the aging wooden slats. The house was over a hundred years old and in dire need of a remodel and a modern makeover. She made a living buying dilapidated old houses, repairing and fixing them up to sell for a decent profit.

Amy and her crew worked hard, sweat glistening on their exposed skin from the sultry summer weather. The abandoned house was stuffy and, without most of the old insulation, hotter inside. Amy bashed away at the slats, letting them splinter and scatter across the barren wood floor.

Normally, Amy went after houses that didn't need this kind of extensive remodeling. She gravitated towards the foreclosures that needed new carpeting, wiring, a fresh paint job, and curbside landscaping. The quick flips, as she referred to them.

This old house seemed to call to Amy with an irresistible siren song, leaving her crew scratching their heads. Her husband, Rick, wasn't too thrilled when he saw how dilapidated the house was, claiming that she was wasting her money and the time of her crew. Amy grumbled to herself as she leaned on the sledgehammer handle as one crewman came up and spoke to her.

"How long do you think it will take for this job?"

"I'm not sure. There could still be more undiscovered pitfalls to be found, Don," Amy replied as she blew a matted clump of hair from her face. "Case in point: the attic with the numerous rat nests."

Don nodded as he reached down and opened an Igloo cooler and pulled out two bottles of water for Amy and himself.

He dramatically shivered while making a disgusted face as he said, "Don't remind me. I think that I still have the remnants of those nasty nests stuck up my nose."

Amy chuckled as her twin brothers, Jack and Mark, came down the rickety staircase, their shirts drenched in sweat and grime. The twins both took off their tool belts and sat down on a stack of plywood.

"Tell me again how much you love this house, baby sis?" Mark said as he wiped his brow.

Don pulled a couple more bottles of water from the Igloo and tossed them to the twins as Jack added, "You know that there're better houses to flip than this one. This house should've been condemned a long time ago."

Amy looked at her crew and sighed. She had the strange feeling that someone, other than the men in the room, was watching her. She couldn't help but casually search for them as gulped down her water.

Amy ignored the creepy feeling and replied, "I know that, Jack. I'm not sure why, but I felt compelled to restore this old house."

Don snorted. "I highly doubt that even Bob Vila would take on this remodel."

"Only because the man is retired," Amy said as set her sledgehammer against a stud and rubbed the back of her neck with both hands. "Why do you guys care? You all get a piece of the final selling price. Would you rather I have you work for an hourly wage instead?"

"With this house," Mark dramatically waved his hand around as he quipped with a grin, "it might be worth it. The overtime would be astronomical."

"If that's how all of you feel, I can easily make it happen and I'll get one hundred percent of the profit when I flip this house, as well as any other houses in future," Amy said with a deadpan expression, all the while trying to suppress a bout of giggles.

Don's eyes widened. "Speak for yourself, Mark. I'd prefer getting a huge chunk of money when these houses are bought. You can have the hourly wage while I'm laughing all the way to the bank."

"So, how's Rick? Is he still bellyaching about this house?" Jack asked as he pulled out a cigarette. He lit it up and then added, "I have a feeling I already know the answer, but I have to ask."

Amy shrugged her shoulders. "He's not happy about it, but I don't give a damn. I had this business way before he came into my life. I refuse to give it up."

"Fighting again?" Don asked as he chugged down the contents of his water bottle.

"He wants me to completely stop, and wants me to have his children and be a stay-at-home mom. But that's not what I want. I'm my own boss and I refuse to ruin what took me years of blood, sweat, and tears to accomplish just because he's feeling some sort of inferiority complex. It's not like he didn't know what I did for a living when we met!" Amy shouted as she plopped down next to her brothers on the plywood, her face red as a cherry with frustration.

Don was about to speak, but stopped when he felt all the hairs on the back of his neck rise up. He slowly looked around but, with the sun slowly setting, couldn't see anything. For a moment he thought that he saw movement in an old closet, but he shrugged it off as one of the many animals that took up residence within the abandoned house.

"You okay, Don?" Mark asked, concern in his voice. 'You look like you've seen a ghost."

Don laughed nervously as he rubbed the back of his neck. "I'm tired and feeling a bit wiped out. You'll understand one day when you're in your fifties like me. I'm going to call it a day and go soak in my hot tub."

"Enjoy your soak, old man," Jack replied jovially. "Don't fall asleep in it or you'll resemble an actual prune. You're almost there without any help."

Everyone laughed as Don flipped off Jack, grinning as he stepped outside. He strolled down the cluttered driveway towards his old, beat-up, multicolored Chevy pickup. Don pulled out his keys to unlock the door but managed to lose his grip on them. He slowly bent down to pick them up, then froze when he felt a cold hand touch his shoulder.

Don's body trembled like he was stuck outside in the middle of winter with nothing warm to wear. An odd voice that sounded like a little child spoke next to him, "*Hey, mister. Can I get a ride home with you?*"

Don turned his head and saw a little girl who couldn't have been more than eight years old touching his shoulder. She seemed pale, with dirt covering her skin in places like she had been playing outside all day. She had dark black hair in pigtails and wore a black and blue dress.

One thing Don noticed were her eyes. In the darkening night they appeared to be black, but he wasn't sure if it was a trick of the shadows from the diminishing ambient light or if she had been in a fight. As she kept contact with him, Don's head felt heavy like he had been given a sedative. His eyes glazed over as he smiled at the child and said, "Where's home, little one?"

"With you, mister. Will you take me home?" the girl answered coldly.

Don nodded. "Sure. You must be famished from playing all day. Marge will have supper ready when we arrive."

Don stood up and unlocked the truck door and slid onto the leather bench seat. He looked back at the child but saw that she wasn't there. He felt confused until he heard a little rap on the passenger side window.

"Will you let me in, mister?" the black-eyed girl asked, her voice devoid of any emotion.

Don reached over and opened the door for her and replied, "Of course. How else can I get you home? Come on in and buckle up."

When the black-eyed girl effortlessly slid into the cab of the truck, the temperature dropped dramatically. Don shook as he stuck the key into the ignition and started the engine. He cranked up the heater and then pulled out onto the street, his eyes still glazed over.

Amy hung her head with her arms resting on her knees. The twins looked at each other, feeling uncomfortable. Jack rubbed her back as he said, "I'm guessing a divorce is out of the question?"

Amy huffed, clearly exasperated. "He's an attorney who works for a huge law firm downtown. He has all the resources at his disposal to ruin and bury me. He's said as much when I tried to broach the subject of divorce."

"Sounds like grounds for a divorce to me. Maybe Mark and I should pay him a visit and let him know how we feel about his attitude," Jack stated as he looked over at his brother.

"He's not worth it. Besides, he'd find legal reasons to ruin you both if you tried anything," Amy replied bitterly as she stood back up, her muscles already aching. She turned around and said, "Let's call it a day, guys. I'll lock up behind you."

Mark stood up and asked, with concern in his voice, "You sure that we can't come over to your place? We'd be happy to be by your side as you tell Dick Rick off."

Amy doubled over, laughing. She looked at her brothers and said, "I'll be fine. Go on and go see your wives and kids. Make sure to give them hugs for me."

Jack stood up and walked over to his sister and hugged her. Mark joined in and said, "Will do, but if you need us call us no matter what time it is."

"I will," Amy said as she let go of the twins.

She backed up and watched her brothers grab their tool belts and walk out the door. Out of habit, Amy locked the door so no one could come in while she was securing the house for the next day.

One night while working late on a remodel, Amy heard a commotion coming from the living room. She came down from the attic and found a couple of young men trying to steal her equipment. Amy surprised them as she rushed towards the thieves, screaming like a banshee while spraying fire at them by using a butane torch and a can of WD-40.

Amy had put too much of her hard-earned money into her business. She felt the need to keep her equipment, as well as herself and the crew, safe from vultures looking for a quick buck at her expense. She walked around the old house, checking the windows as well.

Jack and Mark walked to their vehicles as they joked with each other about the different ways to cause Rick grief. Jack gave his brother a fist bump and went over to his car. As Jack unlocked the door he felt a strange sensation come over him, like he was being watched.

He turned around and was greeted by a young boy all in black. The child stood silently before him, his face showing little emotion as he said, "*I'm lost. I don't know where I am. I can't find my mommy.*"

Jack dropped down on his haunches to get eye level with the boy and said, "It's okay. I can help you find your mom. Do you know what street you live on?"

The boy replied, "*Center Street.*"

"What do you know! I live on Center Street, too. I'm heading home now. Would you like a lift?" Jack said.

The black-eyed boy looked at the man and asked as he pointed at Jack's car, "*Will you let me in?*"

"Sure, squirt," Jack said as he walked around and opened the passenger side door. "Hop up front so you can show me your house."

He turned around just as the boy touched his arm. It sent a cold shiver throughout Jack's body, like a cold front appeared from nowhere and enveloped him. Jack tried to shake it off but nothing seemed to help. He looked at the black-eyed boy, who was already in the front seat, as it asked, *"Will you take me to your house?"*

"Sure, my wife will be able to help me find your family," Jack said as he closed the door. He walked around to the driver's side and got into his car. His eyes were clouded over as he started the engine, his breath easy to see in the air as he put the car in gear and drove away.

Mark unlocked the trunk of his hatchback and rearranged the mess that his work gear made. He haphazardly tossed in his tool belt, not really caring if the contents fell out.

One of these days I'll get a few crates so this won't be an issue, Mark thought to himself, but ended up chuckling out loud.

He never followed through and his work space, no matter where it was, always looked like a bomb exploded. Miraculously, Mark could always find what he needed, something that irritated both his sister and his wife.

He whistled the *Dexter* theme song as he pushed a red tool box to the back of the trunk. Mark closed the trunk with a loud thud as he watched his brother's car speed away. For a moment, he could have sworn that there was someone in the front seat with him.

Mark walked around to the driver's side door, unlocked the door, and got in. He held his foot on the brake pedal and pressed the ignition button, the blast of the cool air conditioning making him close his eyes and relax.

Mark breathed slowly as his heated seat automatically kicked on. He opened his eyes just as a light rapping on the window caught his attention. He turned his head as he rolled down the window and asked, "Yes? Did you need something, kid?"

"*I need a ride. Will you let me in?*" A young child no more than ten stood there.

Most of her face was obscured by the shadows of the night and her hoodie. Mark felt an eerie sense of dread as she got closer to him. For the life of him, Mark couldn't understand why the sudden urge to shift the car into gear and peel out of the area was all that consumed his thoughts.

"Beat it, kid. I'm not a taxi service!" Mark snapped at the kid.

As he turned his attention away from the black-eyed girl, he felt little fingers tapping him on the arm. A bone- jarring chill enveloped Mark's body and he found his head turning to face the kid

"I need a ride. Will you let me in?" the child repeated, the cadence of her voice stronger and more forceful.

Mark had a rude remark ready but he lost all control over his vocal cords. It was as if a cold shroud had encased his entire body, and Mark's will to resist the command of the black-eyed girl eroded into nothing. Panic assailed his senses as he looked directly into the obsidian orbs that appeared to pulsate with power.

Mark's hand slowly moved down the door. He watched in horror as his own appendages weren't obeying his own thoughts and pressed the power lock button. He leaned over and opened the passenger side door, never taking his eyes off the strange child. The black-eyed girl seemed to glide around the front of Mark's vehicle, unblinking as she kept him under her control.

She stood at the open door and said, "*I need a ride. Will you let me in?*"

Mark felt his head bob up and down, helplessly agreeing to her demand. The black-eyed girl got into the passenger seat and closed the door. She put an icy-cold hand on his thigh as Mark shifted the vehicle into gear and drove off down the dimly lit street.

Amy finished checking the upstairs rooms and slowly walked down the scuffed-up staircase. Her clothes were soaked with sweat, since the heat on the upper floor was ten degrees hotter than downstairs. As she stepped onto the main floor, a muffled moan caught her attention.

She looked around, but it was too dark and she couldn't see the immediate source of the sound. She pulled out her Maglite from her pocket and illuminated the decrepit old house. Soft scraping sounds were coming from within the kitchen area. Amy licked her dry lips, her mouth parched as she carefully entered the room.

The kitchen was somewhat renovated with refurbished cabinets and countertops. Nothing seemed out of place, which had Amy wondering if an animal snuck its way into the house. Amy heard the shuffling noise again, but this time it was coming from the inside of a small pantry closet.

She gasped when she saw movement in the gaps between missing slats on the door.

Definitely not a rodent! Amy thought as pulled out a ball peen hammer from her tool belt.

She raised the hammer and demanded, "All right, come out of there. I can see you!"

Whimpers from the pantry caused Amy to pause, her ire ebbing slightly. She tentatively reached out and grabbed the door handle and pulled the door open. Before her sat a teenage boy with his knees bent up, his forearms and head resting on them. The kid was sniffling, like he was crying, and his body trembled.

Amy kneeled down, still gripping the hammer, and said, "Hey kid, what's going on? Why are you in here?"

No response other than sobbing.

Amy reached out and touched the boy's forearm to get his attention. His skin felt cold, like he was freezing. As she gave him a slight shake, Amy had the strangest sensation envelop her senses. Her eyes closed and she dropped the flashlight. She felt lightheaded and nearly lost her balance, but the icy grip of the teenager held her in place.

She opened her eyes and saw the teenager staring at her. Through the ambient light from her flashlight, Amy could barely make out his face. His eyes were as dark as night and she wondered if he had gotten into a recent fight. The longer he touched her, Amy felt colder and her mind was a cloudy haze.

"*I'm scared,*" the black-eyed teenager said in a monotone voice. "*Will you take me home with you and keep me safe?*"

"Who hurt you?" Amy asked.

"*Those that don't care for me. Will you take me home with you?*" he replied vaguely.

Amy stood up, though she didn't understand why she did, as the black-eyed teenager held her by the forearm. She felt bewildered, but the dinging from her phone caught her attention. Amy reached into her back pocket and pulled out her cell phone and saw that the texts were from Rick.

Rick: *Are you done playing in the trash house yet?*

Rick: *I'm hungry so hurry up and get your ass home!*

Rick: *I'm being patient with you, Amy. You really should consider giving up that "job" of yours and staying at home. I can and will support our family, whenever you decide to begin one with me.*

Amy sighed as she sent a quick message saying that she'd be there in ten minutes, and put the phone back into her back pocket.

She looked at the teenager and said, "I'm not sure that you'll be welcome in my house. My husband is in a foul mood, but maybe you can talk to him about who's hurting you and get some legal advice on how to proceed."

The black-eyed teenager reached up and slowly caressed her cheek and jawline, causing Amy to shiver and gasp as he said, "*You're a nice lady. Will you keep me safe?*"

"I…" Amy stammered under his influential control. "I will…do whatever…I can…"

The black-eyed teenager asked once more, "*Will you take me with you?*"

"Yes…" Amy breathed out. "Just need…to lock up…before we go…"

The black-eyed teenager let her go and effortlessly glided out of the house without making a sound. Amy rubbed her temples as she grabbed her keys and slowly walked towards the front door. She wondered when exactly the kid got into the house and how long he'd been in there.

Amy tried to open the door but it was still locked. She was confused as she unlocked the deadbolt, wondering how the kid got out of the house without unlocking it first.

Is there an opening in the house that I didn't notice? Amy wondered to herself as she stepped outside.

She walked over to her truck and used her fob to unlock it. The teenager stood silently next to the truck, but didn't get in.

"Will you let me in?" the black-eyed teenager asked.

"That's why I unlocked the truck," Amy said as she reached over and opened the passenger side door for him. "Get in and I'll take you back to my place and we can get this all sorted out."

He got inside the cab as Amy walked around to the driver's side. When she got into the cab, Amy could see her breath and noticed a lot of condensation on the windows. She rolled the windows down and used a rag to improve her view through the windshield.

As Amy started the engine the black-eyed teenager sat next to her, their legs touching. Her senses were cloudy, like she had taken sleeping pills and her body was fighting sleep. The boy never looked at her as they silently drove down the road.

Amy couldn't help but wonder who had abused the boy and if they were out searching for him. Before she could ask, the black-eyed teenager said, "*I have no one. People want to hurt me. Will you be my new friend or will you be like the others?*"

They turned onto Main Street as Amy replied, "I would never consider hurting you. Um, what's your name? I'm Amy, by the way."

The black-eyed teenager thought for a moment before saying, "*I was never given a name, only pain and suffering.*"

Amy felt her heart breaking for him. "I'm so sorry to hear that. Would you like a name? I'd like to call you by something other than referring to you as a kid."

"*Will you give me a name? I don't understand the meaning of it. If it means so much to you, then pick something that you like,*" the black-eyed teenager said with little emotion.

Amy stopped at a red light and said, "Rick is going to need a name if he's going to help you, so we need to call you something. How about...Greg?"

"*Greg it is,*" the black-eyed teenager said. He finally looked over at Amy. He delved into her troubled thoughts like flipping through the pages of a well-worn book and asked, "*What is the significance of Greg? What was Greg to you?*"

As the light turned green, Amy replied, "He was my first boyfriend back in high school. We did a lot of fun things together."

"*Why are you sad when you say this?*" Greg asked.

Amy bit out, trying not to cry, "He died..."

"*Murdered, you mean?*" Greg stated impassively.

"Yes. He loved helping people in need. He picked up a hitchhiker one night and was found dead in his house, along with the rest of his family. The police never found the person responsible for it," Amy blurted out, not fully understanding why as she sped down the road. For some strange reason, she felt like the black-eyed teenager was drawing out her darkest tragedies. She sniffled and chose to ignore it.

Maybe both our traumatic pasts make it feel like he's safe to talk to about it, Amy mused to herself.

She turned down a side street that led to a private gated community. Amy always felt like an outsider when she went to her home. Rick had bought the house shortly after they got married, claiming that it was the only home she would ever know. He met Amy while she was at a local bar, blowing off steam from a long day of work.

Rick was a charming and handsome man, managing to get her phone number that night. As time went on in the relationship, all was going well as he showered her with luxurious gifts.

All that changed after the couple got married two years later. Rick seemed to slowly shift his attitude, doing little things to get Amy to change her lifestyle and conform to what he wanted her to be, which was a trophy wife.

Fighting and heated arguments were a part of their daily life, because Amy refused to yield to his unrelenting hounding. Rick wanted children and firmly believed that it was his right and her duty to give them to him. Amy rolled down her window to punch in the code to open the gate, the humidity hitting her full force.

As the gate slowly slid open, Greg said, *"Will you keep me safe?"*

Amy rolled her window back up, pressed down on the gas pedal, and said, "Of course I will. What makes you think that I would let anything happen to you?"

The black-eyed teenager remained silent as the vehicle crept down the quiet, well-kept street. Amy turned up a smooth driveway that was neatly lined with various flowers, solar-powered lamps, and small hedge bushes and parked next to a sleek, black Lincoln Town Car. She put the truck in park and got out, with Greg following behind her.

Amy stepped up to the elaborately decorative oak front door and unlocked it. As she stepped over the threshold, she looked over her shoulder and saw the black-eyed teenager standing outside.

"What's wrong, Greg?" Amy asked.

Greg answered, his breath visible as though it was the middle of winter, *"Will you let me inside?"*

"Yes. I didn't bring you all the way out here just to leave you out on my porch. Come on in."

Greg smirked ever so slightly, his black eyes glowed as he entered the house. She closed the heavy, ornate door and turned to escort Greg inside. He placed his hand on the small of Amy's back as they walked through the small foyer.

"Is that you, Amy?" Rick called out from his study.

Amy felt lightheaded and her thoughts were jumbled and confusing, but she managed to reply, "Yes…Where are…you?"

"The study. Where else would I be, woman?" Rick retorted as he stepped out into the hallway in a huff.

He paused when he saw that his wife wasn't alone. He narrowed his eyes as he pointed at the black-eyed teenager with disdain, demanding, "Who the hell is this? A new employee or some stray charity case?"

Amy withheld a groan. "This is Greg and he needs—"

"Need, need, need," Rick spat with disgust as he interrupted his wife. "Everyone wants some damn handout these days. Let me guess, he needs a bed to sleep in for the night? Money?"

Amy was about to speak, but the black-eyed teenager stepped out from behind her. She somehow heard Greg's voice in her head: *"He's going to hurt me. Stop him."*

Rick's eyes widened as he got a good look at their guest. Amy quietly walked by as her husband asked, "What the hell is wrong with you, boy? What's happened to your eyes?"

Rick got closer to Greg and grabbed him by his arms, examining his visage closer. The black-eyed teenager grinned, revealing razor-sharp teeth similar to a shark, and said coldly, *"Don't do that. You're hurting me. It's time for you to go to sleep."*

Confused, Rick stumbled backwards as he let the teenager go. He fell down on the floor, fear lacing his words as he spoke, "W-What are you? G-Get out of my house!"

"You can't make me leave. I was invited in by your wife. I'm not going anywhere, but you will be," Greg replied as Amy sat down and straddled her husband.

The black-eyed teenager put his hands on her shoulders as she stabbed Rick in the chest repeatedly as she growled, "You won't hurt Greg ever again! I lost him once and I'm not going to let you take him away from me! No one will!"

Blood spattered all around each time the blade slipped into Rick's torso. Amy laughed hysterically the whole time, her eyes glossing over and turning gray as she shouted at her dead husband, "You can't tell me what to do, Rick! I love my life and my career! You'll never get me to be a submissive little bitch to show off to your stuck-up partners at the firm! Do you fucking hear me, Rick? Speak, asshole, speak!"

Greg watched from over her shoulder and said with the soft voice of a lover, *"He's sleeping fitfully now, Amy. Let's go to the shower and get you all cleaned up."*

"Okay, Greg," Amy replied, breathing heavily from her murderous workout. The black-eyed teenager assisted her to her feet and walked behind her, still keeping a cold hand on her back. Amy wore a euphoric smile, with Rick's blood covering her face and clothing while still holding the knife as they entered the bathroom.

The black-eyed teenager helped tug her jeans and panties down as Amy reached out and turned the water on in the shower. She kicked off her shoes and let Greg slip off her socks. Amy's eyes were completely clouded over and bordering on being black.

Her mind was trapped in the memory of her late boyfriend and the fun that they'd had together. The black- eyed teenager pulled her bloody, grimy shirt off as Amy worked on unfastening her bra, almost giggling with hysteria.

"Damn, I hope my parents don't come home early from church. I don't know how to explain this!" Amy said as she dropped her bra and entered the shower with Greg right behind her, still fully dressed. "I've never done this before. Are you sure that it's safe to do it here?"

"*Don't worry,*" the black-eyed teenager said coldly, keeping contact with her skin with one hand to better control the memory as the water from the shower head cascaded down her body. His other hand maneuvered her arm and positioned the tip of the knife over her heart. "*No one is going to catch us, Amy. Just relax and enjoy it.*"

"Be gentle. I want to savor this moment with you, Greg," Amy purred as she reached back to touch him.

The black-eyed teenager smiled malevolently as he replied, "*As do I, Amy. Here it comes.*"

Amy let out a small gasp as Greg shoved her body roughly against the wall, causing the blade to plunge into her chest. Instantly, Amy's eyes cleared up as she collapsed in the tub, looking up at the black-eyed teenager in utter shock, and bit out, "Why..?"

Greg replied as Amy died, "*Because you invited me in. I had to take your life, just like I did when your Greg picked me up along the highway. Sleep well knowing this, Amy.*"

The black-eyed teenager stepped out of the shower, not bothering to turn off the water. He walked out towards the front door to step outside. He left the front door wide open as he strolled over to Rick's black Lincoln Town Car. He looked around the quiet neighborhood for a moment and then roughly bumped the luxury car, setting off the alarm.

As swift as death itself, the black-eyed teenager hid in the shadows.

Emergency lights lit up the quiet neighborhood like it was Christmas as onlookers watched from their windows or porches. Everyone was gossiping and pointing as the police and EMT crews worked both inside and outside.

Several officers put up the caution tape and created a perimeter around the house. Detective Barnes stood over Rick's lifeless corpse, taking notes on a little notepad.

"What is with tonight, Jason?" Detective Corbin asked his partner as he stepped up beside Detective Barnes.

"I don't know, Nick. This makes the fourth murder/suicide in one night. Definitely strange," Detective Barnes replied. He looked at Nick and asked, "Have we found a note or anything like that yet?"

"No. It's just like the other ones," the other detective said.

"Either there's some sick bastard out there doing this or we're missing something,"

Detective Barnes said as he scratched his stubbled chin. Another officer came up and handed a plastic file box to Detective Corbin.

Detective Barnes leaned down on his haunches, looking closely at the victim. "I'm not seeing any defensive wounds on Mr. Shiller. I'm fairly confident that his wife did this to him but still, something about this doesn't sit right with me."

Nick let out a low whistle and said, "I believe that we have our first clue, or rather an odd coincidence."

"What do you got?" Detective Barnes asked as he stood back up and shuffled over next to his partner.

"Tax forms and a bunch of recipes, but look at this list here," Detective Corbin said as he handed it to Jason.

Detective Barnes examined the list closely, his eyes widening in surprise. "All the people who killed themselves worked for Mrs. Shiller? Huh, there's got to be some reason for this. Her husband worked for a huge law firm. Maybe someone is sending them a message?"

"If that's true," Nick said with disgust, "then they forced these people to kill their own families and then coerced them into offing themselves. That's either one sadistic crew or we're missing something else. It doesn't make sense."

"Guess we know who we'll be paying a visit to in the morning. Hopefully, Mr. Shiller's law firm can give us some solid leads. I gotta smoke and think about this," Detective Barnes said to his partner as he walked away. He turned his body, trying to avoid the different crime scene specialists and the coroner as he stepped outside.

Detective Barnes jogged over to his squad car and leaned against the door. He liked doing this out of habit— smoke and nonchalantly scan the perimeter of the crime scene for anyone that may stand out in the crowd.

Gawking rich folks, the detective thought as he shook his head slightly.

Watching the crowd, Detective Barnes caught sight of a young teenager intently watching him from next to a light post. He couldn't quite place it, but there was something off-putting about the kid. As the detective snuffed out his cigarette, the teenager approached him without making a sound.

"Sorry, kid, this is an active crime scene. I got to ask you to step back behind the yellow tape," Detective Barnes said sternly as he pointed to the onlookers.

"*I witnessed what happened here, sir,*" the black-eyed teenager said with a hollow stare and monotone voice.

The detective looked at the boy with suspicion, wondering if he was making it up just for attention, and replied, "Is that so? Tell me what you saw."

"*It's not safe here,*" the black-eyed teenager said coldly as he pointed at the police car. "*Will you let me in there so I can tell you everything that transpired tonight with Mrs. Shiller and the rest of her construction crew?*"

All the hairs on Det. Barnes' neck stood on end as he raised his eyebrows. He felt cold as his mouth went dry, wondering if this strange kid had the missing pieces to this murder/suicide puzzle.

How did he know about the other victims?

Detective Barnes turned and opened the back door of his patrol car and said, "Hop in, kid. Let me get you someplace safe. Where are your parents?"

"Dead. I was living with Amy and Rick before what occurred tonight..." the black-eyed teenager said as he touched the detective on his hand.

The sensation of an arctic chill coursed throughout the detective's body upon contact. He shook his head, feeling a little lightheaded, and said, "I'm Detective Barnes, but you can call me Jason. What's your name, kid?"

"Greg. Greg Shiller, sir. They were in the process of adopting me. Will you let me in?"

"That's why I opened the door, Greg. Slide in the back so we can talk privately, away from these *vultures,*" The detective said with a slight nod at the crowd.

As the black-eyed teenager got inside, a toothy, malevolent smirk appeared on his pale visage. Detective Barnes slammed the door and got into the front seat. He turned the ignition on and texted his partner that he had a possible witness that he was taking back to the station. He put his patrol car in reverse and left the scene as his eyes slowly clouded over.

About the Author

Joshua Griffith is a Native American Cherokee who loves to tell stories about the paranormal and the supernatural, but adds a twist of humor to alleviate some of the inherent drama and suspense that can make the characters seem more relatable. He grew up in eastern part of Oklahoma, witnessing many strange and wondrous things that went bump in the night. He currently resides in the Pacific Northwest. As part of his path as an energy healer, the author felt it would be a good idea to incorporate some of his experiences into his novels. As they say, there's always a hint of truth even in a good work of fiction so it's up to you to decide which is the truth and which is hot air. He invites you to read his stories with an open mind because these tales are works of fiction, but ask yourself this: Could this really happen?

If you enjoyed *Terror in the Dark*, please do leave a review. I love reading them because they encourage me to get better and keep the stories coming!

www.ingramcontent.com/pod-product-compliance
Lightning Source LLC
Chambersburg PA
CBHW070831250626
47159CB00003B/725